An Acceptable Future

L.P. Masters

Third Edition: 2023

Second Edition:2019

First Printing: 2018

ISBN 978-0-9982989-3-1

L.P. Masters

www.lpmasters.com

Dedication

To my sister, Kaylene. Thanks for the idea that opened this whole universe to me, or rather, all of these many universes.

Contents

1. First Time

Paul Osmund stepped into Alissandra Goetz's office for the first time.

Again.

Alice tried to remember how many first times it was now. All she could recall was the fact that she'd lost track... at fifteen thousand.

She put on a practiced smile. He returned her smile with a slightly less-angry frown than normal. That was a big step. Maybe things would go well this time.

"Hi, Miss Goetz. I'm Paul Osmund. We had an appointment."

Alice reached over the desk and shook his hand then started to quote the words that were popping into her head, like lines on a readerboard. "I was very impressed with your novel, Paul, uh." She glanced up. "May I call you Paul?"

The analysts told her their reasoning for this question. He liked to be called Paul, but he liked to be asked. He got offended if she just presumed to call him by his first name.

"Of course. Should I call you Alissandra?"

"Alice. Please." Alice looked back down

at her copy of his book. "This...Raynes character. He's so intense, so deep."

Paul's smile widened. *He modeled Raynes after himself*, the analysts blabbered in her head. She wanted to roll her eyes and say *shut up, I know that*, but she sweetened her smile instead.

"Thank you," Paul said.

Alice went on complementing Paul on his brilliant book. She hardly paid attention to what she was saying anymore. All she had to do was quote the analysts. Some days she wondered why she was even there at all.

She'd tried to solve the problem on her own when this all got started, but Paul kept turning her down. After a while the analysts had offered their help. Somewhere along the way it had gone from them helping her, to them simply calling all the shots.

Two years. Well, almost. Twenty months now that she had been stuck in this office. That wasn't day in day out kind of work. That was this very moment played over, and over, and over...

And over.

She was going to snap. She consulted her memory chip to refresh herself on how many times it had actually been. One hundred and sixteen thousand rewinds.

"Of course, the advance and royalties are both negotiable," she went on to say. "We want to make sure you're happy, Paul, and well taken care of. So what do you say?"

He bit his lower lip and Alice's stomach tied in knots that went all the way to her throat. She could feel the heat rising on her cheeks. She had seen every expression on his face before. She could read him as easily as she could read his book.

"Well, I don't know. I appreciate your interest in the book, Alice, but I don't think I'm ready to—"

"Damn it," she muttered.

"Excuse me?"

Alice narrowed her eyes at him. "Damn it," she said again, louder. "And damn you! This whole entire circus is nothing but a—"

"Circus?"

The analysts were going crazy in Alice's head.

"Yeah." Alice stood up from her desk and pointed at the door. "Get out."

Paul's eyebrows folded together. She read his look. Shock. Dismay. How could someone speak to him in such a way? He was about to tell her off, but she wasn't going to let him get a word in. "Out! Now!"

Paul sucked in a deep breath, his chest

rising, his blue eyes widening, ready to start yelling, and then he froze in that position.

Alice groaned. She hadn't sent the command to stop time. It must have been Robertson. She pressed her palms into her eyes and dropped back onto her chair. "I can't even get into an honest fight!"

"This isn't some hologram or simulator program," Robertson's deep voice boomed behind her. "Even though we don't follow every timeline through, Paul still *exists* in every alternate universe we are exploring. Your job is to find the Paul that will accept the contract. You are shaping a man's life here, Alissandra, changing the course of history for the better."

Alice peeked through her fingers as her approver, Robertson, leaned against her desk. He would have the final say in this scenario. Alice had wanted to give up on it months ago because she knew Paul would *never* agree to the publishing contract with Lutrisk Press. Most works of literature were produced by Artificial Intelligence those days. Publishers had plenty of AI produced literature to feed the galaxy's reading needs, but human-created work was rare. It had intrinsically high value.

According to Robertson they were

playing a two-sided game. Paul was going to be influential in the future, not only through the publication of his novel and several subsequent ones, but through his public speaking as well. Lutrisk Press would apparently play a role in the most important publication of the future, but if they didn't get Paul's book deal, they would go bankrupt before the momentous publication could take place.

Alice took a deep breath and looked back at Paul, who stood frozen in time, his mouth stretched open in a shout, his face twisted in rage. She shook her head. "Call the project, Robertson. It's never going anywhere."

"Trust the analysts. This is their job. There *is* a timeline in which Paul will go with Lutrisk. The Darkest has seen it. *Your* job is to find that line and get it pulled into the Universal Consciousness."

Alice had a vague idea of what Robertson was talking about. She'd gone through a crash course when Robertson asked her to do this job so long ago. Apparently there were millions of alternate universes, but there was only one of those universes that everyone seemed to be aware of. That one was called the Universal

Consciousness.

The group that had hired Alice to acquire Paul's book were called the Darkers, and they "improved" things by pulling in the best pieces of history from all the other timelines and incorporating them into the Universal Consciousness. The Darkest was the only one of the Darkers who could change the perception of past and future for the Universal Consciousness. She didn't pretend to understand all the convoluted workings of the Darkers. She'd signed on with them for one project. Robertson had ensured her it would be simple, and after that she could retire with more money than she dared to imagine. Young and rich. She was looking forward to it.

It was anything *but* simple. Not only did she now know about the endless spiderwebbing lines of time, but she had a Temporal Control Chip, or TCC, implanted into her brain and a million other programs she could access at the speed of thought. Her "simple" project had taken 20 months of reliving the same eight minutes, and she still didn't have Paul's signature on the contract.

She grabbed her Lillypad reading device and pulled up Paul's manuscript. She had only gotten through the first three paragraphs before Robertson interrupted.

"What are you doing?"

"I'm an acquisitions editor at Lutrisk Publishing, Robertson. At least, that's what I was nine hundred *thousand* minutes ago before I agreed to help you. And as acquisitions editor, I have to ensure that the work is even any good. You do realize, it was written by a *human*. It could be littered with errors." She'd scanned the book when the query first came in, but she had never actually read the whole thing. She had just jumped at trying to snag him before anyone else could.

Robertson curled his upper lip. "How long is that going to take?"

"Does it matter?" She nodded in Paul's direction. "He's not going anywhere."

"How long?"

"I'm a fast reader. Six hours tops."

She got another few lines in then glanced up at him. "Have you ever read it?"

"No."

"Why not?"

Robertson rolled his eyes. "I hate reading."

2. Last Time

Paul walked into her office again for the first time. Maybe for the last time. If Alice didn't convince him this time she was going to quit.

If you could quit, she grumbled to herself. Robertson said she couldn't quit until she was done. At first that part of the bargain hadn't bothered her. She was sure she could land the deal in a couple of tries and then she'd be rich for the rest of her life.

Now the fact that she'd agreed to work until Robertson declared that they had reached an acceptable future freaked her out. Maybe she would spend a lifetime trying it. Two lifetimes. She didn't know how many lines there were. She had already burned through thousands and Robertson didn't seem concerned about running out anytime soon.

Don't think about it. Just get the job done.

Paul took a breath and was about to introduce himself. Was about to tell her he had a meeting with her. She didn't let him. She'd played this game enough; she was going to take the reins.

She stood up and shook his hand. "Paul Osmund? Alice Goetz. Thanks for coming."

Paul stood there with his mouth open a second, then snapped it shut and nodded.

"Please. Have a seat."

He sat.

"Let me be clear with you," Alice said. "You have a masterpiece on your hands."

The corner of Paul's lip tipped up just a little.

"You could sell this to *anyone*."

The analysts started yelling at her and Alice made a quick mental command and shut them off.

"I don't know anything about any of your other offers, but I'm sure they're in the millions for the advance, with royalties of up to sixty-two percent, am I right?"

Paul bit his lower lip. Alice knew she was right; she'd lied when she said she didn't know anything about his other offers. Robertson had showed her what they were up against. What she quoted to Paul was the lowest offer he had received yet.

Well, other than what Lutrisk wanted to give him.

"Miss Goetz, I appreciate..."

"Please call me Alice."

The interruption seemed to break his train of thought, just as Alice had hoped. She held up a hand to stop him from saying anything more, because she already knew he was trying to say no.

"Raynes," she said, looking down at her Lillypad and scrolling through the pages she had just read. "He's impressive. Brilliant, really."

"Thank you," said Paul, then took a breath to tell her no.

"But Natalie..." she paused to think about Natalie. Throughout the entire novel the tragic heroine was focused, determined. She sacrificed *everything* in order to reach her single goal. She even sacrificed the only true love she had ever encountered, pushing Raynes out of her life so she could have the future she was determined to achieve. And then, just minutes before she accomplished it...

A tear slid down Alice's cheek as the details of the shocking death scene came back to her mind. And yet, even to the very end Natalie had maintained that determination. Her ending was tragic, and yet her actions made it beautiful beyond description, and she achieved more with her death—that ultimate sacrifice—than she ever would have achieved with her life.

Alice drew in a long shaky breath and wiped the tear from her eye, inwardly groaning, and cursing herself for being such an idiot. As soon as she finished reading the novel, Alice knew what she had to say to get Paul to take her contract. Now she was bawling about Paul's incredible writing.

"Natalie is beautiful, and misunderstood," Alice said in a subdued tone. "You need an agent who understands her, a publisher who will respect her." She paused. She was using information Robertson had given her about the future. A big no-no, but she didn't care. "If you sign with *any* of those other publishers, they're going to make you change her, Paul. They'll completely erase who she is, what she does. Her sacrifice will be superficial and meaningless."

Paul's eyes dropped a little, but he didn't try to speak.

"We can't pay you what the others will." She couldn't offer more than Lutrisk was able to pay. Even though she wanted to give him the millions he deserved for the book, she had to make sure to keep Lutrisk out of bankruptcy. "But we want to make this promise: Natalie Case will be untouched and unchanged, free to shine in her intended glory for thousands of years in the future. Everyone who reads this novel will be affected by her. Everyone who reads this novel will search their own souls for what it means to want a certain future... and to *fight* for it."

She didn't know the details, but she knew enough about the future to realize that one woman would take this to the extreme. She would be almost the identical copy of Natalie Case, although her story would thankfully end a little more happily.

Alice leaned forward across her desk and looked Paul right in the eye. "I want to represent *A Failure of Futures*. I want Lutrisk to publish this novel for you, for the universe. It's going to make a change greater than you can even imagine, Paul. So what do you say?"

Alice held her breath, but she didn't release her gaze from him. *Say yes, say yes, say yes,* she repeated, like she could somehow influence his decision with her mind alone.

Paul held her eyes for several seconds. They were breathtakingly blue, and a little piece of hair hung over his forehead, pointing right at them. He was handsome, with a strong, expressive face and a dimple in his chin. Finally he broke eye contact with her and looked down at the name tag across her desk. He glanced back up at her and smiled, and Alice read something on his face that she had never read before, an expression she had not seen in two years of repeating this interview.

He said, "Yes."

Alice quit holding her breath and almost choked as the air hit her lungs again. She felt dizzy and giddy, and absolutely shocked.

"Finally!" She snapped her mouth shut and hoped he didn't notice, then searched her desk for the contract. For the pen. It had been two years since she'd even had to think about either of those.

Her hands were shaking as she held the contract out to him, and she dropped the pen before he could take it.

He picked it up and signed.

3. Forward Motion

Alice had to get used to living her life like a normal human being again, day in and day out, continuously moving forward without stops or rewinds in time. She had to do her actual job again, and she had almost forgotten how to. She was, after all, the acquisitions editor for Lutrisk Publishing. This "job" for the Darkers as a TCC employee—or a Tic, as the more professional Dark Jumper employees referred to her—was supposed to only be a temporary thing. It had been harder than anyone expected to get Paul to sign the contract.

Now that Lutrisk had signed Paul, the hard work Alice had to do was entirely different from what it had been with the Darkers. There was no focus on acquiring new work. Everyone had their full attention on Paul. He was the prince, the VIP, the center of everyone's attention. This was the part where most human authors started to get a big head. Alice had only acquired one other author for Lutrisk since she'd started working there, and the moment Lia Stone signed the contract she'd turned into a lunatic, making unreasonable demands and acting like she was the daughter of the Universal King or something.

Paul wasn't that way, and it was refreshing. He still seemed a little dazed, though. Maybe the pride monster would rear its head when the book actually came out. Whatever. Alice would be done with publishing and retired early when that happened.

Alice still had meetings with Robertson every once in a while, but he seemed pretty happy with where things were headed. He said they were on track for an acceptable future, he just wanted her to stay on the job until Paul was actually published and everything was finalized.

It was probably a good thing she stayed on. Lutrisk had gone through every content editor they had on staff, and Paul had declined every one of them. Alice had asked him out to dinner so they could discuss his options. Maybe she would have to repeat that night a few times if things didn't go well, but it was a nice restaurant. She probably wouldn't mind.

"Thanks for dinner," Paul said as he set his menu down and submitted his order. He looked across the table at her. "I actually wanted to talk to you about something."

Alice nodded. "I need to talk to you, too."

"Okay. You extended the invitation, you go first."

"Let's discuss these editors," Alice said. She pulled her Lillypad out. She'd downloaded all of the sample edits, and she had gone through each one, looking for the strengths and benefits each editor offered. "Sarah can really improve your structure. She's great with looking at the overall story and clarifying any plot issues."

Paul grinned at her. "Yeah. But she sucks at spotting the grammar stuff."

"We have a proofreader for that."

Paul shrugged. "I don't know. I just don't click with her."

"Then how about Terrence? He's great with grammar, and he can straighten out any confusing paragraphs in the novel."

"He's way too aggressive. I felt like I was back in grade school, and my teacher pulled out the red pen and marked at least one thing in every sentence. Honestly, I think his commentary on the sample was longer than the novel itself."

Alice looked at Terrence's edits on the Lillypad and had to agree with Paul. It was maybe a little over-the-top. "Fine. But Cameron's edits are—"

Paul started to laugh and Alice stopped talking. She glared at him.

"What?"

"I said you could go first, but now I'm wishing I hadn't been so kind."

Alice furrowed her eyebrows and pursed her lips. She had no idea what he was talking about. An AI waiter brought their meals and Paul said thanks, even though the robot didn't care about manners.

Paul pushed his plate to the side and leaned toward Alice. "I wanted to ask if you would consider being my editor."

Alice's mouth fell open, but she didn't say anything.

"You are, after all, the only person in the universe who truly understands Natalie. And you promised me she wouldn't be changed."

"She won't be!" Alice assured him. "That's already been made clear with all of the editors Lutrisk has sent your way."

Paul smiled. "Maybe so. But I just don't trust them."

"Well why should you trust me? We've only met twice." Alice felt like she knew him intimately for how many times she had rewound that moment in her office, but for Paul, it was only twice. She'd made a few calls to him, but talking to a holographic image of a person was not at all like meeting them.

"Twice is enough," Paul said. "I already know I want you as my editor."

"I haven't even submitted a sample."

"That's okay."

"But I might be like your grade school teacher. You don't even know."

"That means you're thorough."

"What if I suck at grammar?"

Paul smiled. "They have proofreaders for that."

She shook her head. "You don't make any sense. How can you look at fifty-two sample edits and not like a single one of them, but you can assume that I'll do a good job without even seeing my work?"

He raised an eyebrow. "I don't know. Like I said, I just trust you."

He infuriated her. This was the most important publication Lutrisk would ever have, and he wanted her to edit it based on some unfounded idea of trust. "No." She said, and leaned back in her chair, folding her arms. "You need to pick one of the editors."

"Really?"

"Yeah. Really."

"Well I don't want one of them. I want you."

Alice clenched her jaw. She knew this was stupid, but she wasn't going to be bossed around by him. Sure, he was an author, and he was the most important thing Lutrisk had, but her answer was no. "I won't do it."

Paul stared at her for several seconds, the look on his face a combination of shock and frustration. "Then I'll make you do it," he said. "How about that?"

"Try."

Paul looked like he didn't really want to do this, but he was pulling his last card. "Fine. I'll annul the contract then. Go somewhere else with the book."

"No you won't. Once a contract's signed, you're in."

Paul laughed. "Have you seen the lawyers lately? You read about that lawsuit with Fredrick Laughman, I'm sure."

"Those lawyers cost more than you could pay them in fifteen lifetimes."

"Not if I get a different publisher to pay them for me."

Alice took a breath and looked down at her food. It was her favorite dish at this restaurant but it suddenly didn't look appetizing. The steak was bleeding.

"Just do the edits for me Alice, and everyone will be happy."

"After you've forced me to have no choice?"

"You've forced yourself."

He was so annoying, and he didn't even know it. "No," she said at last.

"What is wrong with you?"

Stop. She sent the command to her Temporal Control Chip, and Paul froze in time. She ran this scenario as far forward as her Chip would allow, but Alice was only given a window with the TCC. She only had four hours to play with. That meant she could back up four hours, and look four hours ahead, but that was it. Looking ahead didn't usually help much, but that time it showed her that Paul did indeed leave, and he went straight to Sogodon Publishing, asking for legal help with getting out of the Lutrisk contract. Of course they said yes. They were saying yes before he was done asking the question.

Rewind.

"Thanks for dinner." Paul set his menu

to the side and submitted his order. Alice was still looking for something different to eat. She had the feeling she would never be able to look at her favorite meal the same again.

"Alice," Paul reached out and pulled her menu down. "I need to talk to you about something."

Every time Alice changed timelines, she "changed Pauls," as Robertson put it. Alice wasn't actually going back in time, she was just changing what universe she sat in. There were multiple universes with Paul in them, but every one had different influences, and had created a slightly different Paul. This man sitting across from her had lived an entirely different life from the man she'd sat with last time.

"Actually, I needed to discuss something with you as well," she said, trying to get out of it.

Paul grinned. "Well I spoke first, so I go first," he said.

Alice's stomach dropped and she was pretty sure she went pale. She knew what he was going to say. And then he did. "I want you to be my editor, Alice. None of these others will do."

"Oh, come on!"

Paul had a half-smile on his face but looked confused. "What?"

Alice dropped her menu and leaned forward. "Paul, I haven't edited anything in years. I'm in acquisitions. I read stories for potential, I read for strong characters and plot. I don't edit."

"But you can. You went to school for this job, I'm sure, and there were editing classes."

"The same kinds of classes all the other editors went through. Just not as many."

"I don't care. I don't want them, I want you."

She rolled her eyes, "Well you can't have me."

Paul chuckled. "Why not? I'm a human author. I can have whatever I want, can't I?" he said it with a joking tone, but she didn't like the idea of him pulling the author card on her. She'd heard that one too many times with Lia Stone, and Lia had always won with it.

"No. You can't have me."

He took a breath to yell, and Alice stopped him.

Rewind.

"Be my editor."

Rewind.

"There's no one else who can do it."
Rewind.

"Without you, I know I'll be nothing."
Ugh! Rewind!

Each attempt she made to convince him that he didn't need *her* as his editor failed.

Stop, she said after another failure, and she looked forward to see what would happen in the next few hours.

He killed himself.

Wow. She didn't expect that. Different universe, different Paul, but still, even just seeing it made her sick.

"What the hell are you doing?"

Alice jumped at Robertson's deep voice and spun to see him.

"He wants me to be his editor."

"Then be his damn editor. You give him whatever he wants, Alissandra."

Alice frowned.

"Let me see," Robertson mentally reached out to her TCC and Alice granted him access to the last few recordings. He watched them in a fast pace that made her head spin. Anytime someone else accessed the TCC-contained memories, she relived them, too.

"Sounds like he wants you," Robertson said. "What's the problem?"

"I don't do editing."

"Well now you do."

"Robertson, I—"

"Do your job, Alissandra. We're paying you to bring him through to final publication, not to get him to sign a contract and then leave in the middle. Lutrisk has spent too much money on him already; you'll put the company under even faster. And without us to support you when they fall, you'll be out of a job, and have the reputation in the publishing world as the woman who lost Paul Osmund's contract for Lutrisk."

Alice took a deep breath. Robertson was right. She nodded. "Fine."

"Now just remember; these universes aren't infinite. They're created from the choices your subject makes. Don't go around destroying dozens at a time simply because you want to change an answer that isn't going to improve the future."

Alice wanted to say, *I don't know about that. Have you seen my editing skills?* But she didn't. She was lying to herself about her editing skills being bad. The truth was, even though she didn't *want* to edit, she was good at it. Paul was probably right in his selection of her as an editor. The singular thing she refused to admit was that she didn't want to be Paul's editor because it was too intimate.

The last time she'd worked with a writer on his editing project, she'd fallen in love. She couldn't help it. She loved literature, and she loved writers. When she put them together, and worked closely with them, she completely lost her head.

She glanced at Robertson and wondered if she should mention that danger. She'd been warned not to get into any kind of personal relationship with the subject. What Robertson didn't realize when he told her to take the job as Paul's editor, was that he was nearly forcing her to break what he said was the most important rule of the job.

Alice still remembered when he told her not to fall in love. He'd almost gotten emotional. She had the feeling he'd broken the rule himself, and the memory of it was still painful.

You can do this. You can do an editing job without losing your head.

Yeah, sure.

"Fine. No more unnecessary rewinds. I'll be his editor if he asks this time."

"Good girl," Robertson said, then he

submitted the rewind himself.

"I've never been to this place. I'm excited," Paul said, still perusing his menu.

Alice set hers down and stared across the table at him, trying to find all the things that annoyed her most about him. She had to look for that kind of crap now, just so she could remember when she started to fall for him. He had this little piece of hair that fell in front of his left eye all the time. He was constantly pushing it back. She didn't understand why he didn't just pick a different hairstyle. The one he wore was outdated, anyway.

She didn't get a chance to find any more annoyances before Paul said, "You've been here before. What would you suggest?"

The first thing that popped into her mind was her favorite dish, despite the fact that her first try at this meeting had ruined her from ever liking it again. "They call it the Station King. Best food you've ever had."

Until a writer goes and destroys that for you by asking you to be his editor.

Paul smiled at her. "Thanks." He pressed the button for the voice-order and said, "Two Station Kings, please."

Alice sat there, resigned to what was

about to happen. He would ask her to edit for him. She would be doomed to say yes.

They didn't say anything for a few minutes until Paul looked at her and asked, "So what did you need to talk to me about?"

She was flustered. He was playing hard to get. "Well, we need to find you an editor, Paul. We have offered literally everything we can."

Paul sighed and nodded. "I know. I've been through those sample edits countless times, I just..." he trailed off.

"What?" Alice asked.

"None of them *feel* right." He tapped his fingernails on his teeth. Great! Another thing to annoy her. She filed that away.

"Paul, you don't need this book to be perfect. It's the imperfection that people are drawn to when it comes to human created art. Originality is imperfect by necessity. Don't look for the editor that you think can make it perfect, look for the one that you think will make it better."

The waiter came by with the food and Paul looked up at it. "Thank you." He drew in a deep breath through his nose and said, "Wow, Alice. This looks amazing."

She nodded, and looked down at it. It really did look amazing, and in all of her rewinds she still hadn't taken a single bite of food. She decided if she had to go forward with time, no more rewinding, then she was going to have to eat.

She cut a chunk off the steak and put it in her mouth. Flavor flooded her taste buds and she closed her eyes, enjoying the meal more than she ever had before.

Paul's chuckling shattered her enjoyment of the moment and her eyes flew open.

"What?" she asked.

He grinned at her. "Nothing. I just haven't seen someone enjoy their food that much in a long time."

Alice glanced around, wondering if anyone else had noticed her pleasure. She thought back to all the times she had been there, all the people who might have seen her eating, and she suddenly felt very self-conscious. She set her fork down.

"Anyway. As I was saying, we need to find you an editor." She pulled out her Lillypad. "Now, I think Stacey might be your best bet." Alice had already gone through every option with him during her many rewinds. She knew all the concerns he had with them, and he was least concerned with Stacey.

"You think Stacey?" he asked.

Alice nodded and leaned forward. "She's easy-going, so she won't somehow remind you of, I don't know, your grade school teacher leaking red all over your assignments. She's got a great handle on grammar, and she can pick out plot problems from a mile away."

Paul nodded and leaned back in his chair. "Okay."

Alice's heart started beating faster. "Okay?" she asked, leaning even further into the table. She'd been expecting him to refuse her suggestion and demand she do the editing.

"Yeah. Okay," Paul said. "If you think that is honestly the best option I have for an editor. If you think that is the person who will treat Natalie the way she should be treated, then I'll trust you. Because you were the one who promised me that Natalie would be protected."

Paul leaned forward too. Their faces were only a few inches apart across the table. He said, "I haven't said anything to you about it, because I don't want to be too forward with you. But I think you would be my best option for an editor. You know the story, you know Natalie more intimately than maybe even I do. You can give me the edit that no one else would be able to."

He shrugged and sat back. "That's what I think, at least. But you're the professional, so you tell me. What do you really think is best for my book, best for Natalie? If you say Stacey, then I'll believe you."

Alice nearly fell back in her chair. She couldn't believe it. He was giving her an option, a chance to say no. She leapt at it. "I really do think Stacey is the best..."

She couldn't say it. If Paul's book really held as much weight in the future as Robertson said it did, then it needed to be as good as it could be. Alice was the one who could bring it there.

She sighed. "Fine. You're right. Natalie needs me. But I will only do this on one condition. You remember that this is a professional relationship. Nothing personal happens between us, is that understood?"

"Of course!" Paul looked surprised that Alice was even bringing it up. "What else would you expect?"

Alice rolled her eyes and didn't answer that question. She didn't want to expect what she expected.

4. Forgotten Kiss

It wasn't Alice who fell first. In fact, she kept congratulating herself on how well she had kept her distance from Paul as she worked on the edits. She kept pretending that the work she was reading and enjoying so much was just another piece produced by an Artificial Intelligence. It was a hard lie to believe. It was a spectacular story for something produced by a computer.

That worked well until Paul called her up and asked to go through some of the edits. He had a few questions that he wanted answered.

Alice tried not to cringe as she said "yes," then she looked around the mess in her office and tried to clean up quickly before he came.

Twenty minutes later he was sauntering into her office. The atmosphere, the way he held himself was completely different from the thousands of times he'd stepped into her office when she was trying to win the contract. Now he was confident, strong. He sat down across from her and said, "Okay. Did you look at those passages I mentioned?"

"Yes."

Alice had known he would disagree with her suggestions when she was making the edits. She'd known what passages he was going to bring up the moment he'd called her.

"So... really? You want me to take the metaphor out?"

Alice licked her lips and tried to keep the smile off her face. She nodded.

"I know I said that I trust you, Alice. But this is a little crazy. Do you have any idea how long I worked on that metaphor?"

"Yeah. I do. And it shows. You took five sentences to get through it."

"They were short sentences."

Alice shook her head. "It doesn't fit there." She grabbed her Lillypad and pulled up the edits, leaned across her desk and torqued her body to get close enough for them both to see the page. "Just look. Let's work through this together. Trust me—like you said you do—and you'll understand in a couple of minutes."

Paul sighed. It sounded like he was annoyed, but the look on his face told Alice he was interested in what she was about to say. She went on. "Okay, so take a look at this. If you pull the metaphor and just tell the reader how it is, the paragraph is going to be a lot cleaner."

He shook his head, "But the metaphor explains it in more depth than you could get just by saying it."

"You don't need depth. Not here." She highlighted the metaphor and cut it. She saw Paul's body tense in her peripheral vision. "Stay with me, Paul," she said, putting a soothing hand on his arm, then said, "Okay, let's move on..."

Alice got so caught up in her work that she completely lost track of time. She didn't care. She wanted to get to her point, even though that was a few hundred pages further in the book than where Paul had come in with his edits. As she glanced at the energy in Paul's expression she got the idea that he didn't mind the long work.

At last they got there, and Alice smiled inwardly. "All right. Here." She tapped the screen where she wanted to talk about, and Paul leaned in closer to read. His shoulder brushed against her arm, and he shoved that piece of hair out of his eyes again. She could smell his soft musk. "Yeah?" he said. "So what?"

"This is boring. This part of the book is

boring. Raynes is basically saying the exact same thing you were saying back a hundred pages when you dropped that metaphor."

Paul didn't say anything, but his eyes seemed to light up. Alice pasted the metaphor she had cut earlier, and changed a few things before and after to make it fit. "When you've led up to it with all those other changes we were just doing, then all of a sudden it's—"

"Beautiful!" He was looking at Alice. "You're brilliant, you know that?"

Heat flashed across her face and she shook her head. "You're the one that came up with the metaphor. I just changed where it was placed."

She tried to put her focus back on the book, back on the edits. She wanted to get away from that look of admiration on Paul's face.

"Anyway. I was thinking the word *sprouted* sounds better than *grew* here, when Raynes is talking about..."

"Absolutely stunning."

Alice glanced at Paul and made a face. He was staring at her. "Are you still talking about the metaphor?"

Paul grinned. "Metaphorically speaking, you could say that." He paused. "But what I really mean is you, Alice."

Without any other warning, he leaned in and kissed her. The breath caught up in her lungs and for a moment she considered pushing him away. She didn't do it that first moment, and after that it was too late.

She didn't want this to stop, but part of her knew that it must, and immediately. Robertson had told her over and over not to get involved with a subject. When he first started bringing it up, Alice didn't think it would ever be a problem. She only saw Paul as an annoying, stubborn writer who refused to sign his novel to Lutrisk, no matter what she tried.

Now all of that had changed. She had found a way to separate Paul from his writing using that little mental trick that it was AI produced. She was sure she didn't like him just for his writing; there was something about him that kept him on her mind. He's the kind of guy you meet once, but he jumps in your head incessantly.

You've met him a lot more than once.

That was true. Maybe she was falling for him just because of his familiarity. Maybe that was the exact reason the Darkers told her not to let it happen.

So don't let it happen. The money was

more important to her now than falling for some writer. It never worked out. She'd been with writers before, and after the last time she'd vowed not to let it happen again. Now not only was she going against what the Darkers told her, she was going against what she had promised herself.

She pulled away from him and was instantly left with a feeling of emptiness. She wanted to linger just another few seconds, so she rested her head on his shoulder and tucked her face into his neck, filling her nostrils with his scent. She was screaming at herself that she should never have let this happen.

"Alice," Paul whispered in her ear, his voice as soft as his comfortable scent. "I think... I love you."

Alice jerked back from him. "What?"

"I'm sorry. I know it's abrupt, and I shouldn't feel this way. I promised to keep it professional, but it's like... it feels like I've know you for years." He paused, brushed a strand of Alice's dark hair behind her ear and said, "I love y—"

She couldn't let him say it again. His first pronouncement had been hard enough to take. She shoved him so forcefully that his chair tipped over and he began to fall backward. "*Stop!*" she screamed at him. Her command was so emotional that it translated to her Temporal Control Chip, and Paul froze in time mid-fall.

No. She wasn't going to fall for a writer again. She took three deep breaths and looked around. The analysts were gone. Robertson wasn't around much anymore unless she was screwing around with time like she'd done at the restaurant. One rewind might not draw attention. Besides, she had no other choice. She sent the command and watched everything backwards.

Seeing herself tuck her face into Paul's neck, Alice realized that it looked bad. Even though she'd gotten mad at him after he told her he loved her, she was cuddling up to him before that. What would have happened if he hadn't ever dropped that bombshell? She was sure Robertson would ask that same thing if he ever saw the experience.

The TCC reached the end of its reverse movement ability. She didn't realize she'd spent four hours with him on that editing. She was too late to tell him she couldn't work on the book with him, but she at least could tell him to move the metaphor without going through all the edits in between. It's what she should have done in the first place.

Alice took a deep breath then accessed the Chip's memory control. She watched the last four hours in forward motion, memorizing the edits she made that would now have to be re-made. As the file came to the end, she listened to the last words Paul said before she stopped time.

"I love y—"

Her heart was pounding, and part of her wanted to whisper, "I love you, too."

Instead she whispered, "Delete memory file."

The TCC obeyed and the file was wiped from its memory banks. No electronic memory of the kiss remained, and for Paul, it never would have happened.

But Alice's brain wasn't electronic, and it wasn't linked to time. She remembered that kiss. She was afraid she would remember it for the rest of her life.

5. Almost Done

Alice had opted to do the editing sessions long distance since the forgotten kiss. She and Paul spent a lot of time looking at holograms of each other while they scrolled through pages on their own Lillypads. They'd finished edits on the whole novel that way, and in a very professional—and unemotional—way.

Paul couldn't kiss a hologram.

It had been three days since she'd even talked to him. Now that the editing was done, there was no reason for them to speak. The typesetters were working on formatting, and the next day the company was throwing a launch party. Paul would get his advance, and Lutrisk would officially be Paul's publisher.

Robertson had held a meeting with Alice—outside of time, of course—and told her that she was nearly done. They were on course for an acceptable future. He just wanted her to stay with it until the book was officially published then she could be off the job. She would be paid, and she could live her life however she wanted. As long as she stayed away from Paul, that is. Robertson made sure *that* was clear.

She couldn't be finished with this job soon enough. Even though she rarely saw Paul, she couldn't get him off her mind. When it was all done she would go to some tropical world and find some incredibly handsome boyfriend to take up all her attention. At least *he* wouldn't have that strand of hair constantly falling into his eyes.

But the strand was becoming a little less annoying, and a little more endearing every day. It constantly brought attention to the deep blue color in his eyes, and she found herself staring at those so much she didn't notice the hair. And when he smiled, the only thing she could see was that cute dimple in his chin.

Alice groaned at herself as she walked toward the office. Getting off the planet might not be good enough. If she'd told herself a few months ago that she would feel this way about Paul, she wouldn't have believed it. After hearing him say no a million times, she never would have imagined that by the end of it, she would miss him.

But she did. Terribly. Ever since the kiss

she'd stayed away from him, even though all she wanted was to see him again.

A block away from the office, her phone rang. It was Paul. Her stomach fluttered and she considered rejecting the call for a moment. Instead she tapped her ring where her call controls were and answered. "Hello, Paul."

His full hologram appeared beside her. If it weren't for the occasional flicker of her second-rate holo-ring, it would have looked like he was walking along beside her.

"Alice! The proof copies came today. They're sitting in a box on my kitchen table."

That was Lutrisk's thing. Anyone could sell electronic books, and Lutrisk certainly had their fair share of books for the Lillypad, and every other reading device. Paul's would be available there, as well. But any time they got a contract for a human-created novel, they published it in print. A traditional form of publishing for a traditional way of writing, they liked to say.

"How do they look?" Alice wanted to see the books. She'd only seen a few print books in her life.

Paul shook his head "I don't know. I haven't opened them yet."

"What? Are you crazy?"

"Probably. I wondered if you wanted to open them with me?"

Alice couldn't help the smile that rose up on her face. She shook her head as if to tell herself no, but that didn't seem to help. "Of course I do."

"Great." He paused. "I sent you my address."

A notification popped up beside Paul's hologram with the address he'd given. Her holo-ring had already calculated the distance there and the estimated time to travel.

"I'll catch a RAT and be there in ten minutes," she said, already working to hail one.

"I'll be waiting."

Paul's hologram disappeared while Alice hailed a Robo Auto Transport. She slid into the RAT and shared Paul's address with its guidance system.

Alice bit at her lower lip as her personal memory of the kiss they'd shared popped into her mind. Something in her gut told her the excitement she and Paul shared for the proof copies could easily translate into a different kind of excitement.

She refused to believe that. She'd

worked hard on that book, and she deserved to be one of the first people to ever see it. She could control herself. She had to control herself.

Everything would be fine.

6. Proof Copies

"Another glass?" Paul asked, holding the bottle of wine toward her.

Alice wasn't much of a drinker, and she knew she shouldn't have had wine with him in the first place. When she got to his home, she'd tried to just look at the books and leave, but Paul had insisted that they celebrate. He'd asked her join him for a bottle of wine he'd been saving for this very moment. She had been weak when she said yes.

No more weakness. Alice shook her head and tucked her feet up under her as she readjusted in her chair. "No thanks. I've already had too much."

Paul looked guilty a moment, his eyes shifting around the room as if to see who was watching, then he poured himself another glass. Alice couldn't help but laugh at him.

As he drank, his eyes fell to the book in front of him, and he set the glass aside, picking up the novel and staring at it.

Alice picked up her own copy. It was *hers*. Paul had already signed it and given it to her. The cover was beautiful. The man they had chosen as the model for Raynes fit Alice's mental picture of him perfectly. The woman they picked to model Natalie bothered her a little, though, and she couldn't say why at first, but in the few hours she'd spent celebrating and drinking with Paul, it started to come together.

Natalie looked like Alice. They had a similar body type, both had straight dark hair, heart-shaped faces, even the bright brown eyes that looked almost orange instead of brown. Those were all the attributes Paul had written about Natalie in the book, but Alice had never realized how much alike they must have looked.

She started to realize how much in common she really had with Natalie. Alice didn't want to admit her feelings for Paul, but even without admitting them, she knew they were there, and she knew they were not allowed. Robertson had made it clear that if she got involved with Paul, it could threaten the future they had worked so hard to achieve.

Just like Natalie, Alice wanted something specific out of her future. And just like Natalie, Alice was going to have to sacrifice the man she loved to achieve it.

Paul's voice cut through Alice's

thoughts. "Are you okay?"

Her eyes snapped up to him. Her worrying must have shown in her face. *Just rewind it now,* she told herself. She should have rewound a long time ago. There was a window. She couldn't go back any further than four hours, and she already knew that she was too late to go back before she accepted Paul's offer to see the books. If she didn't act quickly she'd be too late to turn down his offer of wine.

Rewind now.

"I changed my mind, Paul," she said, then held her glass out towards him. "I do want some more wine."

Paul poured more and Alice put the glass to her lips. It took all her self-control not to down the wine in one gulp.

Are you going to rewind?

Not yet.

She kept thinking of that kiss she'd shared with Paul. She was the only person in all the universes who remembered it. She knew it was careless, but part of her wanted to see if he would kiss her again. It would be easy enough to back it up again and erase it like before.

Alice set her glass on the table again and looked down at the cover of the book.

Paul took her hand in his. "None of this would have happened without you, Alice. I mean, I didn't even realize how important Natalie was until you..." He trailed off, and looked at her so she could read that same expression she'd seen the last time they kissed.

She was ready to dive right in. Ready to kiss him again. Ready to do almost anything.

And then what? Rewind? Make everyone else forget it while she carried it for a lifetime, knowing she wanted him but could never have him? This had been a bad idea.

"Paul, I'm not supposed to..."

He didn't let her finish. He leaned across the table and kissed her on the lips. It was a quick kiss, a testing kiss, as if he wasn't sure how she would respond. So very different from the last kiss that had been confident and passionate.

Even still, it filled her with so much desire to be with him that it nearly took her breath away. She would never be with him. He would never remember this moment. Oh, why hadn't she rewound? It would have been easier if she didn't have to deal with this. Her look of anguish let him know she wasn't ready for the kiss and he sat back.

"I'm sorry," Paul said. "I know this is abrupt. We've only been working together a little while, but I feel like I've known you for years."

He'd said the same thing last time, and it was very shortly followed by "I love you."

Alice shook her head. "No, I'm sorry, Paul. I shouldn't have let it go this far."

His face fell to what Alice recognized as rejection, hurt.

"This is supposed to be a professional relationship. We can't—" She took a deep breath and covered her face. All she wanted to do was kiss him again. She dropped her hands and leaned across the table toward him. "You won't remember this kiss, Paul. I just wish I could forget it, too."

"What?" he asked. "Are you screwing with my mind or something?"

"No." Alice shook her head. "Not with your mind."

She was about to give the mental command for her TCC to stop time, but the word came from a different voice.

"Stop."

Paul stood up and stepped over to her chair, kneeling down in front of her. "Tell me the truth, are you manipulating me in some way? Some kind of mind control?"

"No." If she could control his mind, none of this would be happening right now.

"I have no reason to feel the way I do about you, Alice, and I know that. I've only known you a little while, and if you think about how many times we've actually met, it isn't very many. But I..."

He was going to say I love you.

"Don't, Paul," Alice said. She shook her head. "I don't want to hear it."

"No." He stood up and grabbed the bottle of wine from the table. "I know you don't want to hear it. I'll see you at the launch party tomorrow."

He turned and walked away, swaying a little as he went. He was probably drunk. They'd already finished one bottle together.

Alice should have just left, but she knew that this timeline would continue, this Paul would continue. Every Paul she interacted with came from somewhere and would go somewhere. That was the reason why she couldn't tell any of them about her ability to manipulate time, even if she was about to rewind and change what line she was on.

Without explaining her other job, there was no way she could explain what just happened. How could she explain her wanting him, him wanting her, but she refused to let it happen?

"I'm sorry, Paul."

"Yeah. You go and be sorry," he said, spinning around to confront her, but he turned too hard and stumbled.

The bottle shattered as Paul landed and he cried out in pain.

Alice rushed to his side, her eyes danced across the multiple cuts and slices, trying to find out how seriously he'd been hurt. It looked bad. There were severe gashes that ran the length of his arm. Blood mixed with wine on the floor. He was already going pale.

Come on, Alice, Rewind it now! She couldn't bring herself to do it. This man would continue in time, even if Alice didn't. She couldn't just leave him there.

"Paul!" Alice didn't touch him. She wasn't sure what to do.

He shook his head, and a tear trickled from his eye. "Guess I'll be even more famous now." He chuckled weakly. "The artist dies before his... book..." he trailed off and looked up into her face a long time. When he spoke again, his voice came out a hoarse whisper. "I... love..."

You. Alice finished his last statement in

her head, because he never did. His body slacked, his head lolled to the side. His deep blue eyes were no longer seeing.

"Paul? Paul!"

A notification popped up in her TCC. *Subject Paul Osmund of line 52719 no longer shows signs of life. Please rewind and select a more acceptable timeline.*

Alice wiped her tears away. Yes. Paul was dead. But there was another Paul who was alive. People who worked for the Darkers saw death all the time. She shouldn't have let it affect her like that.

She sniffed. She had caught a scent a moment ago. Through the tangy sweetness of blood and wine she could smell something else. Something with a sweet spicy smell. It was familiar, and she could almost place what it was but not quite.

Stop, she commanded the TCC, and all the scents disappeared. Everything outside of time was always muffled. The lights seemed a little dimmer, the voices of people speaking outside of time sounded a little duller. The smells were completely gone. It felt unnatural. Alice hadn't really paid much attention to it when she was trying to get Paul to sign the contract, but now as she looked around the dim room she wondered if that was the reason they called themselves Darkers.

She looked down at Paul and heaved a deep sigh. She was ready to rewind and erase again when a deep voice said, "What the hell have you been doing?"

Alice's gut clenched. She spun around to see Robertson standing behind her, his arms crossed over his chest, a deep frown on his face.

"I'm sorry," Alice whispered.

"Let me see your records," Robertson demanded.

No time to delete it now. Alice granted him access to her TCC and felt the uncomfortable sensation of having someone rummaging through her mind. She could see everything he could. Images from the week before flashed through her head. A dark spot blinked for a moment at a deleted memory, then more images played again.

Robertson stopped, backed up.

"What's this?"

The memories filled her physical mind, but thankfully he couldn't read that. A kiss, an 'I love you' that didn't end with Paul dying.

She pulled the deleted file, inspected it. "I'm not sure," she lied. "Must have gotten corrupted."

Robertson glared at her, then looked at Paul's body on the floor. "I told you not to get involved with a subject."

"I know," Alice shook her head. "This afternoon was an accident. A fluke. It was all Paul's fault. I don't feel the same way about him." She hated herself for blaming it on a dead guy. Hated herself for lying, but she had to. The truth was, if she didn't have this job with the Darkers, she'd be with Paul in half a second.

He narrowed his eyes but didn't say anything to her. "You know what happens if you fail?"

Alice shivered. The Darkers had showed her what the future would be without the influences Paul and Lutrisk put on the universe.

"I won't fail," Alice said. She opened her rewind path choices with him. Robertson could make choices on which path she took. When Alice rewound, the computer made those choices for her. "Tell me which line has the best options available."

"You're too late to refuse his invitation here," Robertson said.

"I'll leave as soon as I see the books."

She felt like a school girl in front of the

principal. He studied her face as if he had learned to read her as easily as she'd learned with Paul. Maybe he was searching for truthfulness, wanting to know if she actually *would* leave.

"Would you like me to take you off this project?" Robertson asked.

She wasn't sure if it was a question or a threat. "No. Please. I want to see this through." She shook her head. "I'll distance myself, I'll just watch and make sure everything is progressing properly. Really. I'll be fine."

Robertson's face softened a little. He took a step closer to her. "The TCC chooses what path you'll take based on your goals. When you wanted Paul to sign the contract, it searched for the most likely lines in which he would sign the contract."

Alice nodded. She knew that, but it apparently didn't work very well, considering how long it took to get that contract signed.

"When you want *him* the TCC has a harder time of it. It confuses your goals with the goals of the Darkers. You know when all of this is over you can't have him. You know that, don't you?"

Robertson wasn't even touching her,

but she felt like he was strangling her. Her words were the whisper of a whisper. "I know."

He nodded then turned around and started to leave. He waved over his shoulder to where Paul's body was. "Get this mess straightened out, Alissandra. No more fooling around."

She nodded even though his back was to her, and watched him disappear into some other time line. Robertson never stepped into the flow of time. Alice wondered if that meant he would live forever, if it meant he *had* lived forever, but something about the way he talked made her think the Darkers had a limit. It obviously wasn't a *time* limit, but they always worried about how 'long' things would take.

Alice was ready to rewind but then she glanced back at Paul again. She walked over and knelt down beside him, staring at his pale face.

You can't have him. You know that, don't you?

She broke down and cried.

7. I Have to Leave

"It's beautiful, Paul." Alice looked at Natalie and felt like she was staring in the mirror. Sacrifice everything. Even the love of her life. "I have to leave, though. I have a meeting."

"Oh." He looked disappointed. "Well I'll see you tomorrow, right?"

"Tomorrow?"

"At the launch party."

Alice had hoped to step away from him and never see him again, but he was right. She would be expected at the launch party. She clenched her teeth and said, "No, Paul. I don't think I can make it."

He furrowed his eyebrows, pursed his lips. It was his look for confusion, a little bit of pain tossed in. "Okay. Well maybe you can come over after the party and—"

Alice didn't even want to hear the invitation. She shook her head. "No. I don't think I should."

She turned to leave. Paul snatched a book from the table and chased her. "Alice, wait. This one's for you." He held the book out toward her. "I'll even sign it for you."

She wanted it. She wanted it so badly. If

she couldn't have Paul, at least she could have this reminder of him. But she knew it was a bad idea, and she had been doing too many bad ideas for too long. She shook her head. "No."

"I don't understand."

The look on his face made her want to cry, but she bit her lip and said, "I know you don't. I'm sorry. I..." she looked at the floor where he'd died just moments ago in her memory. "I have to leave."

8. Murdered

Alice's four-hour window turned out to be her doom. If she could have, she would've gone back and changed that last interaction with him at his house. She would have played the right role, showed the proper excitement. She would have left before he tried to kiss her.

It was too late now. She had been rewinding for a full year's worth of time. Even though it had been a year in Alice's mind, Paul still felt the pain of her rejection as if it had happened last night. The launch party was a disaster. He ruined his career at it. Every damn time.

Alice had tried everything. She'd tried showing up at the party and apologizing. She'd tried stopping him from going to the party in the first place, both actively and passively. It didn't matter. He always did something wrong; got drunk and punched the CEO, or said something insulting to a reporter, that would end up going viral.

Sometimes he died before he ever showed up to the party.

That night at his place was the first time she'd seen him die. It wasn't the last.

Sometimes it was an accident; most times it was suicide. Alice blamed and cursed herself every time she cried over another dead body. It seemed to be happening more and more frequently, and it was really getting to her. All she wanted was for him to get through that night alive, and with his career intact.

Alice stood back in the crowd, watching Paul from a distance. He was talking to Shayla Oscar, the well-known book reviewer. Alice's stomach flipped. No doubt he was going to offend her, and that would send this timeline careening off into nowhereland again.

She made a choice. She hadn't approached him and tried to get him to be reasonable in several rewinds. She tugged on the bottom of her shirt and crossed the room to him.

Shayla noticed her first. "Alissandra Goetz," she said. "Another spectacular human find."

Alice had to think hard to remember what Shayla was talking about. Alice had gotten the contract for Lia Stone years ago—decades ago it seemed. Stone's contract was probably the reason why Robertson had approached Alice in the first place. "Thank you Shayla." She glanced at Paul. "Can we talk?"

Paul glared at her, looking like he was ready to say no, so she grabbed his arm and pulled him away from Shayla.

"Did you come to apologize?" he asked.

"No."

Paul looked a little miffed, but Alice had already apologized enough times. She wasn't going to throw herself at his feet just so he could step on her again. Tell her he didn't care when it was obvious that he did. He was acting like a child. But she couldn't blame him.

Alice looked around at the party. The place was dangerous. Pretty much everyone he could speak with was in a position of power, and he offended pretty much everyone he talked to.

"Let's go," Alice said.

Paul scoffed. "I thought you weren't coming to the party."

"Paul." She took a deep breath and closed her eyes. "Don't destroy your career because you're angry at me."

"My career? What are you talking about? I've got the advance—tiny as it is—and the royalties should keep me comfortable enough. Why should I make this a habit? What? You really think I'll write another book? Lia Stone never did."

"I think you—"

Shots rang out through the air and screams erupted from the front of the room. Alice and Paul turned to see the group of black-clad armored men pushing through the crowd, shooting people when they didn't get out of the way. The deafening echo of their guns told Alice they were using bullets, not lasers.

"What's going on?" Paul asked, terror in his voice.

Alice never answered. The leader of the group pointed at Paul. "There he is! The pretty little *human* author. Writing is a computer's job."

The men opened fire and one of the shots took Alice in the chest.

She fell to the ground, pain burning through her body. She rolled over to see Paul who was clutching at his own wound. "Paul," she gasped.

He looked at her and pain crossed his face as he realized that she was dying too. "I'm sorry, Alice. I love you."

She was tired of denying it. And she was dying now anyway. There was nothing more for her now but the truth. "I love you too," she whispered.

The men stood above Alice and Paul and the leader sneered. "Awe. Ain't that sweet?"

Then he shot her in the head.

9. Chain Emotion

Auto-rewind.

Alice gasped and then screamed.

She wasn't lying on the ground, she was standing up, and the conflict between horizontal and vertical made her dizzy. She stumbled forward, caught a lamp post, and sucked in several heaving breaths.

She had never died before.

Someone passed by and bumped her arm. She gasped and spun, backing away, and right into another person. "Hey! Watch it."

Stop, she begged her TCC. *Please, just stop!*

The world fell silent and the people froze in place.

Alice sucked air in through gasping breaths, sobbing.

"What the hell is wrong with you?"

Robertson appeared beside her.

"I died. I died. They killed me."

"I don't give a damn about that. Let me see."

She knew what he would see. "Never mind, it's—"

"Let me see!" he nearly screamed at her.

Alice opened her TCC to him, but she could almost feel him tearing into the programming before she gave him permission.

He ran the memory at several times the speed it actually happened, and Alice watched it replay in her mind; getting Paul away from Shayla, telling him not to ruin his career, the murderers breaking into the party.

She didn't remember the actual sensation of pain in her chest, but watching it again made her hold her breath.

Robertson slowed down at the end, and Paul's words came out at normal speed. "I'm sorry, Alice. I love you."

"I love you too."

The murderer put the gun to her head and pulled the trigger. The memory froze just as the bullet began to burrow into her skull.

Robertson stared at her for endless seconds. "I love you too?" he accused.

"I was in pain," Alice said. "I was *dying*. I had no idea what I was saying."

"You once told me this was all Paul's fault, told me you didn't feel the same way. Well apparently that's not true. How long has this been going on?"

"Robertson, it's nothing."

"Nothing?" he asked. His voice rose nearly to a scream, "*Nothing*? This is *everything*, Alice. This breaks every single rule you learned from the moment you agreed to help the Darkers."

"He'll never remember it," she whispered.

"That doesn't matter. Have you heard of chain emotion?"

Alice stared at the ground.

"Let me refresh you. There are numberless versions of one subject. Generally each version's emotions are controlled by what happens in their particular timeline. They're separate, unconnected. There is a phenomenon, however, that when multiple versions experience the same emotions in enough timelines, the subject begins to experience chain emotion. Why should one man be depressed when his life is perfect and without problems? Because enough of his other versions' lives are so screwed up that he resonates with them."

"I know," Alice said.

"The same can happen with love. Centuries ago people talked about fate, destiny, love at first sight. Most people thought it was a joke. The truth is, it was chain emotion."

Alice didn't want to hear this, but she had to know. "So what are you telling me? That he's in love with me in every single timeline?"

"It would appear so."

Alice bit her lower lip a moment before she said, "Then maybe we're meant to be together."

"You're not," Robertson said flatly, as if there wasn't anything more to say about it.

"What if we are?"

"No one is meant to be with their subject. You have created a completely *un*acceptable future here."

The venom and fury in Robertson's voice made her feel like she had touched on a personal subject. A very personal one. "You fell in love too, didn't you?"

"It wasn't love," he said quickly, then looked like he regretted admitting to it. He frowned. "Just get him through that damn party without him making a fool of himself."

"Is that really all I need to do?" she asked.

"Yes," Robertson said, narrowing his eyes. "That's all you need to do."

Robertson disappeared, most likely going to Darkness; a place that existed entirely outside of time.

Something wasn't right. Alice knew that Paul always offended someone at the party. Robertson kept telling her those offenses led to an unacceptable future, but people got offended all the time. The fact that Paul was a human writer basically gave him a license to be a jerk if he wanted. It was probably expected, to be honest. It was not something that would ruin him. Alice shook her head. Lia Stone had been awful at her launch party.

Maybe Robertson was wrong. Or maybe Robertson was lying. Maybe some of those times he had offended people would have turned out fine in the future.

But why lie when he was so determined to have an acceptable future? Why lie? She went over their conversation again in her head. *No one is meant to be with their subject.*

You fell in love too, didn't you?

It wasn't love.

Robertson had been in the exact same place Alice was; in love, but not allowed to have the one he wanted.

Maybe he would trap her in this four-hour time loop for the rest of eternity, punishing her with an angry Paul, making her watch him die more and more frequently until there was nothing left.

Her stomach dropped. Although the choices seemed endless, Alice knew they weren't. Especially for her. The people who did her job as official members of the company were called Dark Jumpers. They could lay the whole timeline out and choose which one to follow. Alice was dependent on her TCC, and the algorithm for the TCC's choices was set by Robertson's definition of what their mission was. Even if he told her some of this was her fault, he was the one in control. He was the Jumper in charge of her mission.

Alice needed help, but she couldn't go to Robertson.

10. Darkness

She had only been to Darkness once, when she had undergone the strenuous training that was required for her to get the TCC. She didn't belong there, but there was no one who had told her she wasn't allowed to go. She accessed the Chip and told it to take her there, then quickly added, "Away from where Robertson went, please."

Alice never understood what happened when she went to Darkness. Maybe she would have known more if she'd been a Dark Jumper. Some part of her thought it was all in her head, but she knew that couldn't be. Robertson actually disappeared when he went there. Her body must have moved there somehow, but it only took a moment and she was standing in the endless halls of Darkness. The steel walls made the place feel cold, but bright bulbs illuminated everything in white light. It didn't *look* like darkness in Darkness. Somehow it *felt* like it, though. There was an extreme pressure that surrounded her constantly, like she had dived to the bottom of an ocean, with a thousand atmospheres pushing down on her.

Alice looked up and down the hall. The place her TCC had brought her was empty. She decided to go left and she walked until she came to a door. It led to an entertainment room, which was filled with game tables, books, vids, anything someone could want to take their mind off the pressures of work.

There was only one man in the room. He sat on a couch, flipping through a book on a Lillypad. Alice moved in slowly, unsure if she should talk to him or not. She wandered around the room for a moment, pretending to show interest in what was to be found, but her gaze kept returning to the man.

He turned the page and gave a sigh that was an interesting mix between frustration and satisfaction. She couldn't bury her curiosity any longer. "What are you reading?"

The man jumped and glanced over his shoulder at her. "Oh. I didn't know anyone else was here." He looked down at his book again, then laid his finger across the page to mark his spot. He brought up the cover and let her see it. Her eyes snapped to the familiar title, but the image was completely different than the one she was used to.

"It's called *A Failure of Futures*. Have you read it?"

She sounded breathless as she answered. "Um, yeah. I have."

"Love this thing," the man said. "I've read it since I was a kid."

Alice put her hand to her head as a wave of dizziness washed over her.

"Hey, you all right?" he asked, dropping the book on the couch and standing up. He was tall, dark-haired, handsome in a rough kind of way. He looked familiar, especially his deep blue eyes.

"Yeah, I'm all right. All this time stuff just gets to me sometimes."

"I can understand that. When are you from?"

Alice glanced at his Lillypad on the couch then nodded toward it. "Right before that book came out."

"Are you working on Paul's line?"

She nodded, then reached her hand out toward him. "Alissandra Goetz," she said.

The man shook her hand but didn't introduce himself. Instead he glanced around the room and asked, "What are you doing here?"

She bit her lower lip. "What do you

mean?"

"You're just a Tic, aren't you?"

Alice glanced at the door and considered running for a moment. It didn't matter. If this man was going to get her in trouble, she was already in it. He knew her name now. "Yeah. That's right." She took a long breath against the suffocating pressure of the place. "I just... don't know what to do."

"Hmm." He sounded interested. "What's going on?"

"My subject keeps screwing up his career. Or simply dying."

The man's question followed quickly. "How often has he died?"

Alice consulted her TCC. "Eight hundred and seventy-two." The number shocked her. She hadn't realized it was so high.

The man looked disturbed. He searched the room with his eyes.

"What?" Alice asked.

"Have you heard of an ever-fail?"

Bile rose up in Alice's throat. She'd learned about the ever-fail phenomenon when she was in training. Even the best time-scientists couldn't explain the universal dead end, where every choice a subject made eventually ended with their death.

"Yes, I have," Alice said slowly.

"Does it seem like that might be the situation?"

She searched her mind for symptoms and matched them up with Paul's. "Early stages, I'm sure of it."

"Damn it." He grabbed her by the shoulder. "Come on. Let's go."

"Where?"

"The Jump."

Alice stopped walking. The Jump was where all time was laid out like an enormous spiderweb. Anyone who saw it went insane. "I'm not allowed to see the Jump."

The man urged her on, unconcerned. "You'll be fine."

"But I've heard anyone who goes there loses their minds."

"You think every Dark Jumper is insane?"

He smiled at her and the breath caught up in her lungs. He'd seemed familiar, but she couldn't understand why. Now she recognized it. That smile was the same as Paul's.

"Who are you?"

He gave her a knowing look. "My name's Josiah Osmund."

Alice caught her breath. He had to be one of Paul's sons or grandsons. She knew he couldn't be *her* grandson. The Darkers would never allow her to be with Paul. She wasn't sure if she was happy or upset about knowing that Paul would have a family with someone else. Part of her wanted to ask Josiah who Paul married. Part of her knew she didn't want to hear the answer.

Josiah seemed to recognize the look in her face. "Remember," he said, "You came here to stop the ever-fail."

Alice nodded. It didn't matter who was Josiah's mother. Paul had already died on too many lines. In the early stages of an ever-fail, they had to stop messing with timelines and pick one. If Alice couldn't get to a line Robertson would accept, it would come to a point where Paul died over and over until there were no lines left with him in them.

11. The Jump

They walked in silence a few minutes, then Alice asked, "What happens if Paul dies?"

She knew Josiah understood what she meant. What happens if he dies in every timeline? Then Josiah wouldn't have a father or grandfather. Whatever Paul was to him.

Josiah smiled at her. "Those kinds of questions take a full training course to answer."

She knew he wasn't joking. It screwed with her mind that she was even meeting him, but Darkness existed outside of time, which meant Alice could have hung out and had tea with her great-great grandmother if the woman had been a part of this enormous universal secret.

"Here we are," Josiah said, and stopped at a door clearly marked. "The Jump. Authorized Personnel Only."

Alice hesitated at the door, but Josiah smiled at her. "It's fine. I'm authorized."

"Yeah, but what about me?"

"What's there to worry about?"

"Um, if Robertson finds me here, he'll kill me."

Josiah chuckled. "Nah. That's the beauty of being outside of time. You can't die."

She furrowed her eyebrows at him.

He grinned. "You haven't even taken a breath since I told you my name."

Alice realized she'd quit breathing and had simply forgotten to start again, but she didn't feel breathless. She inhaled, more out of habit than anything, but he was right. She didn't need to.

"Come on." Josiah stepped inside and Alice went in after him. It was a small room, and it was actually dark, unlike the brightly lit halls outside. Several computers sat in one corner. There were windows in the walls, but there was absolutely nothing beyond them. At least, nothing that Alice could see with unaided eyes. In reality, what lay beyond those windows was time, stretched and twisting and going on forever. She shuddered as she thought of what would happen to her mind if she saw it.

"Damn!" Josiah slammed his fist down on the desk and Alice's attention snapped away from the windows. She recognized the tree-like diagram of a line map on the computer screen, but she'd never learned to read one.

"What is it?" Alice asked.

"It is an ever-fail." He mouthed another swear word but didn't say it out loud.

Alice shook her head. She wanted to deny it. "But you're here, so that means he makes it, right?"

"Not necessarily." Josiah sighed and stepped away from the computer, leaning up against the wall. "The Darkers picked me to be a Dark Jumper long before they decided to make changes to Paul's book in the Universal Consciousness." He shook his head. "This is where stuff gets really screwed up. I don't know if I can even explain it."

Alice knew she was about to have her mind blown away, but she needed to understand what was going on. "Try," she said.

"You know about the Darkest, right?"

The one person who could change the past and the future, and actually change it, not just move to a different timeline. Alice nodded.

"I know we're outside of time right now, but you have to see this as if there is still some kind of... chronology for lack of a better word."

"So pretend that time still exists?" Alice asked, then chuckled. "I think I can do that."

"The Darkers have the job of finding the changes that will most vastly improve the future of the UC. That means that they're constantly searching for those changes. They might find a change a hundred years in my future and do that first, then find a change a hundred years in my past and do it next."

"Sounds a little chaotic."

Josiah rolled his eyes and nodded. "Time is chaotic. But by doing things that way, they've got to have a way to isolate each of the changes, so that they affect the parts of the UC the Darkers want them to affect, but not the parts that are already good. It's like they're rebuilding a rope, but only replacing the strands that are frayed or messy."

Alice nodded. It made sense, even though it was hard to believe they could do that.

"So yes, I'm Paul's grandson, and the book I read growing up was published by Darmouth Entertainment. The Darkers realized that if Lutrisk published it instead, there would be great improvements in the UC, so they started up that project. I worried about it when I heard they'd hired you as a Tic, but they promised that it wouldn't affect me. They could isolate things enough that I wouldn't be changed. Paul would still be able to follow basically the same line he did before, just with a different publisher. He'd meet the same people, go the same places, marry the same..."

Josiah trailed off then stepped forward and looked straight into Alice's eyes, his tone grew serious. "If something happens to change Paul's line in a way the Darkers can't isolate, though, then they have no choice but to change me."

Alice got his drift. If she fell in love with Paul, then Paul would never marry Josiah's grandmother. What Josiah meant when he said he would be changed, she didn't know, but she could hear the fear in his tone of voice. It wasn't something she wanted to do to someone.

That was why Robertson didn't want her to be with Paul. If he had explained that, though, she would have understood. Looking at Josiah she wouldn't want to do anything to hurt him. She hadn't cared about Robertson's warnings that she couldn't have Paul, but she was ready to listen now that she knew what it could do to someone else.

"So what can we do?" Alice asked. "We can't let him die everywhere."

Josiah shook his head. "I don't know. Once things get rolling in an ever-fail it's extremely hard to stop them. Let me take a look."

Josiah maneuvered the image of the tree around. He scrolled through more lines and ended with a series of curses.

"What?"

"This ever-fail wasn't an accident. Someone started it rolling."

The smell. The spicy-sweet scent she'd noticed when Paul died that first time. She thought she recognized it but couldn't place where. Now the memory came back to her. She'd smelled it the day that Robertson came to her in her office and asked her to get Paul to sign with Lutrisk Publishing. It was the only instance she had ever met him in the flow of time, the only instance she had been able to *smell* him.

"Robertson," Alice muttered.

Josiah tapped a spot on the tree as if it would mean anything to Alice, "He set it off right here. About twelve hours past what your TCC will let you back up to."

Rage built in her chest until she wanted to explode. Twelve hours beyond her TCC. She knew what that was. It was only a few hours after she'd kissed Paul. Robertson was doing this to spite her, to punish her for falling in love.

Josiah shook his head. "There has to be a way out of this." He started searching, manipulating the tree.

Time didn't exist in darkness, but human minds are addicted to the concept of counting it. Alice felt like they were in that room for ten hours. She kept worrying that someone would walk in and demand to know what was going on. She kept worrying that Robertson would be that someone who walked in.

She couldn't believe that he would set off an ever-fail and completely destroy the mission just to keep them apart. But if Paul could marry the same woman who was Josiah's grandmother, then things would be fine. Alice could follow her original plan, get away from him. Maybe she could even set Paul up with the right woman before she left.

"I know it doesn't matter... but who was

your grandmother?"

Josiah glanced at her and flashed a sympathetic smile. "You really love him, don't you?"

Alice didn't answer. She'd already gotten in enough trouble for admitting it once.

Josiah sighed and looked back at the screen. "The scary truth is, I don't remember who my grandmother was."

"You don't remember?"

"No. Which means you're in more trouble than you realize."

Alice clenched her teeth, then relaxed her jaw and asked, "Why do you say that?"

"The first symptoms of a past changing. Whoever my grandmother *was*, I doubt she still is any more. I likely won't remember her until you're done with this mission. Hopefully those are the only changes I have to go through. I've heard change is painful."

Alice took a deep breath and let it out slowly. "Well however it ends, I can't wait for all of this to be over. Then everything will go back to normal."

Josiah frowned. "Well. Pseudo-normal."

"What do you mean?"

He shrugged. "I don't know. Something

just *feels* different when there aren't as many versions of you in the universe."

"There aren't as many versions?"

He tipped his head. "You mean they didn't tell you what happens when you rewind?" His face was covered with surprise, and an undertone of disgust. His was just as easy to read as Paul's was.

Alice shook her head. "No. Please tell me."

Josiah turned away from the screen for a moment and looked at Alice. "They should have told you when you started. This job is not as simple as it seems. Not even for a Tic."

Well, Alice hadn't been told whatever it was Josiah was talking about. It must have slipped Robertson's mind. Or maybe he just didn't care to say anything about it. He didn't seem too concerned with her welfare. "Tell me."

"Many of your other versions are already dead, Alice." He glanced back at the screen that showed Paul's tree, and said, "A lot of them are. Most of your versions on other timelines don't survive long after your consciousness has left them."

Alice shook her head. "I don't understand."

Josiah rolled his eyes. "You understand that time is like a spider web, right? Every major choice creates a new line in time."

"Yeah. I understand that. I'm not actually 'rewinding' time. I'm just moving from one line to another."

"Well, sort of. You're not actually *moving*. Not in a sense that your body is going from here to there. What's happening is that you're transferring your consciousness from one line to another. If you could look at the mind of Alice on line A before you transferred there, you would find a woman who knew nothing about the Darkers and what they can do. The instant you transfer to that line, that Alice knows everything you do."

She shook her head. "So there are thousands of Alices out there who know the truth about the Darkers?"

"No. In fact there are very few. No one has been able to figure out why, but any time a consciousness is transferred to a new line, the line becomes unstable around that one person. Once the consciousness goes somewhere else, that person is usually destroyed. In rare circumstances the line remains stable, and another 'you' continues on. When that happens the Darkers will either tell you never to speak of the truth about time, or they'll simply erase the memories you have of what they do."

"So every time I have rewound since I started this job, I've been killing myself?"

Josiah had a deep frown on his face as he nodded.

Alice recalled what she'd been told when she first started this insanity three years ago. She quoted it. "It's a simple job."

"It *should* have been." Josiah rubbed his face as if he was tired. He looked back at the screen. "I'm almost finished here."

"What are you seeing?" Alice asked.

He frowned. "Nothing good. I'm still looking for something better."

He didn't look at her as he said that. She could read guilt on his face.

"What is it?"

He shook his head. "Nothing. I haven't found the right ending yet."

"Josiah, the Darkers lied to me from the moment I started this job. I don't want you to do the same thing. Please, just tell me."

He looked at her for several seconds then said, "It would be easier to show you."

He touched the tree in several places, then sent the info to her TCC. "These are all the paths you have left to choose from. Now remember, any future vision is nothing more than projections. It could still change. But the programming is pretty accurate. It's usually right."

Alice watched as Paul died again and again. Her mouth dropped open and her stomach turned sour.

The images were still playing in her head as she said, "So is that it? How do we get out of it? How do I save him?"

Josiah stopped the parade of deaths. He rubbed tiredly at his eyes again. Maybe it had been more than ten hours. It wouldn't have surprised Alice if they'd already spent the equivalent of days in there.

"This was all I could find," he said. "The only line that doesn't end with Paul dying, but..."

Just like before. It was easier to show her than tell her.

Alice watched the projection of the future, seeing it as clearly as when Robertson had replayed her murder and her illicit admission that she loved Paul.

As the projection came to an end, Alice wiped the tears from her cheeks then looked at Josiah, trying to put on a face of bravery even though she didn't feel it. "And if this happens, he'll be on the path for an acceptable future?"

Josiah bit his lower lip. "He'll be alive," he said, then frowned. "I don't know how acceptable I'd call it, but the Darkers would no doubt take it. They don't have much choice right now."

She clenched down on her teeth. "Do me one last favor, Josiah. Set this to my TCC as the new goal. Can you do that?"

"I'll take a look, but I don't know if I'll be able to override Robertson's control."

Alice gave him access to the TCC. It wasn't long at all before he frowned and said, "That already is your goal, Alice, but Robertson has set it to require you to go through every other option first."

She knew what that meant. Robertson was forcing her to transfer her consciousness to every single timeline she had left, which meant that her line would destabilize shortly after she left it. Setting this as her goal meant Alice could never be with Paul, and that was precisely what Robertson wanted. If she did this she would be giving Robertson everything he desired.

So be it. She couldn't let Paul die.

12. Pretend You Love Me

Alice dropped into time. The noise and movement of the city were deafening. The buildings rose in the air, most of them in the downtown area were over a mile high. The Sten Lashton building was the anchor for the space elevator, but many of the other buildings had floating parks, high above the hustle of the city. The weather was kept under strict control in the downtown area.

Watching all the bustle of the city, Alice could see how a man could die here; how he could die a thousand times over.

Time. Alice didn't have time to waste. She touched her ring and contacted the publisher's aide that was in charge of Paul's launch party.

"This is James Drew."

"Hi, James, it's Alissandra Goetz, Paul's editor. Something came up. Paul won't be able to make the launch party."

"Something came up?" James sounded infuriated. "What's so important he can't make it?"

Alice rolled her eyes. "A death in the family," she snapped, then hung up.

She set that moment as her auto-rewind

jump point so she wouldn't have to make the call again if she wound up dead in the next few hours.

Well, *when* she wound up dead.

Alice shivered then scanned the crowd and picked him out. She took a breath. Save him. That was all that mattered.

She jogged toward him, "Paul!" she yelled.

He turned and looked at her. His sneer clearly illustrated his disgust. "What are you —"

Orange flames and black smoke licked into the air as the Sten Lashton building behind Paul exploded. The ground shuddered beneath Alice and she fell. When she finally righted herself she was amazed that Paul was still standing. She raced to him, fighting against the flow of panicked citizens running the other way. She had just barely gotten to Paul's side when he dropped to his knees and fell forward.

A steel beam was lodged in his back. It must have been thrown like a javelin at him when the building exploded.

She rewound and started running the moment she got back in time. All that did was get her caught in the fireball, which happened to be bigger the second time around.

The third time, Paul survived the explosion, only to be trampled to death by the crowd running for their lives.

Time and time again Paul died as the lines in this scenario played out, all the lines in which the terrorist group had set their bombs in the Sten Lashton building. She kept trying to save him, and she kept dying right along with him.

Alice rewound, started her race toward him and yelled his name, "Paul!"

"What do you want? You come to appolo-"

"Move."

She dragged him away, ready for the explosion, but it never happened. She was in a different universe, different timeline. Whatever terrorists had planted that bomb didn't exist anymore.

That just meant there were new things to kill him.

Alice had gone over all the things Josiah had shown her, but the TCC refused to link the deaths to the timelines she was in. She wasn't a Dark Jumper, and that knowledge was not permitted. The TCC was supposed to be doing all that work for her. All it meant was that the damn thing would take her through every single one of Paul's deaths, instead of letting her skip to the one line she wanted.

Alice scanned the buildings, the ground, the sky. His deaths could come from anywhere and she knew it.

"What's going on?" Paul demanded.

Alice glanced at him, then turned her attention back to possible threats ahead. She'd noticed something, though. She looked back at him.

His skin was pale and moist. His breathing didn't sound quite right. "Are you all right?"

"I'm fine..." He grabbed his stomach and groaned.

"What's wrong?"

He straightened up, kept walking. "Nothing. I just haven't felt right today."

"No kidding." Alice frowned. "We have to keep going."

Paul took another few steps then doubled over in pain.

"Paul!" Alice cried, real concern sinking through her vocal chords. "What's happening? What's wrong?"

He fell to his knees, curling up into a ball as he groaned.

Stop. The word ran through her head

but she didn't send the command. Someone else had.

"What happened?" she asked, assuming she was asking Paul.

"He was poisoned."

It was Robertson's voice. Alice looked at Paul; he had stopped suffering. He was silent and still, curled in a fetal position on the ground, his face turned toward Alice with a look that read a mixture of things. Pain, fear, pleading for help.

"Poisoned?"

"Early this morning. Long before you have the ability to go back and stop it."

Alice's chest swelled up with rage. "You can't kill him in every line, Robertson! You claim you want an acceptable future, but you *manufactured* this ever-fail."

"Oh. I won't kill him in *every* future. You've seen the end, haven't you? Don't think I didn't notice when your TCC was tampered with."

Alice sneered at him.

"You still work for me, Alissandra, and we will still achieve our future. Don't worry. I'll paint you as the tragic heroine. You'll like that."

She tried to keep the shudder from showing, but Robertson probably saw it anyway. "Everyone will know what you've done, Robertson. Josiah will tell them."

"Josiah. Yes. A very unfortunate thing, really. You see, the future is so unpredictable. Josiah was originally Paul's grandson, by way of a woman named Cheryl. But in a few hours, Paul will be on his way to becoming the man our future needs. You will be... well, you saw. And Josiah will be non-existent. I suppose you'll be happy to know that Paul never falls in love again. He originally married Cheryl, but now he'll have no interest in her. Without you around, there won't be anyone to provide him with progeny."

Josiah would cease to exist. Alice wanted to punch Robertson in the face. She swung for him, but her fist stopped just inches before it hit him. He'd moved her body back into time, now only her head was out. She couldn't do anything but speak.

"But Josiah... the changes he's made... if you destroy him, then what about the future?"

"Oh, the Darkers can find a replacement for him easily enough. They've had to deal with these kinds of problems before. Don't you worry about the future, dear. It will be wonderful."

The Darkers. Were they allowing this to happen? Why weren't they stopping him? "How do you expect to get away with this?"

Robertson flashed a quick smile then said, "I have a friend or two in high places. Once they're done working on the records, no one will be able to know how the ever-fail started."

Alice felt a tear slip from her eye but she couldn't wipe it away. "Why?"

Robertson narrowed his eyes. "Because we're not *allowed* to fall in love with our subjects. And if I couldn't have Malia, then you can't have Paul." He took several deep breaths as if he were filled with rage, then he said, "We're done here. I'll see you at the end."

Alice dropped out of time and gasped as her hand fell to her side. Paul cried out in pain, his face begging her to help.

She knelt down beside him.

"I don't know... what's wrong," he gasped.

"You're dying." She clenched her teeth. "You were poisoned."

"Hospital... quick."

Alice signaled an emergency on her ring and shook her head as a tear tumbled from her cheek. They wouldn't be there in time, but at least she could comfort him.

He writhed in pain again, then looked up into her face. He seemed to realize it was too late as well. "I'm... going to die."

Alice nodded, and took his hand in hers.

"Then... love me. Just pretend. For one minute... pretend you love me."

The tears fell freely then and she said, "I do love you, Paul. I don't have to pretend."

13. Lightning Strikes

Paul died of poison over and over. Alice knew she could have rewound as soon as she realized he was dying again, but she never did. She stayed with him until the end. Every time. It was Robertson's personal torture, forcing her to go through every single line before she could get to the end.

Paul took his last breath again and Alice took a deep breath of her own, closing her eyes and wondering how much more of this she could handle. She'd tried to convince the TCC to choose a different path, but Robertson had strict instructions to the chip in her head. It was running every single line until the very last one. The one line that Robertson had deemed the 'acceptable' future. It meant that Paul would die in every decision except one, and Alice—according to Josiah—would die in them too.

But it was what she had to do. There was no turning back now.

Rewind.

Thunder clapped overhead.

Alice looked up at the towering buildings. Black rainclouds masked the sky and rain fell in bullet-sized drops.

"Alice?" Paul asked.

She studied his face. None of the paleness, the pain she had seen for so long as he suffered with poison. She almost gasped with excitement, then thought better of it.

"What's going on?" She looked up at the sky again.

"What are you doing here?" he asked. "They've told everyone to stay inside. The weather system failed and they couldn't keep the storm at bay."

Alice frowned at Paul. "Okay. Then what are *you* doing here?"

His gaze dropped to the puddles at his feet. "I, uh..." he bit his lower lip. "After what happened last night, I figured..."

A flash lit the dark city streets, and a few seconds later the thunder rumbled again, so loud she could feel the reverberations in her chest.

"Tell me, Paul."

"I figured it wouldn't really matter if I was out in a storm."

She narrowed her eyes at him. "You're trying to kill yourself?" she asked.

"No. Just... not trying to protect myself."

"Well you're an idiot."

Paul looked away and Alice sighed.

"I know I'm an idiot," Paul said. "I'm sorry. It's just... I'm crazy for you, Alice. I have no idea why. And then you treat me like you did last night and..." he trailed off.

Last night? It felt like a decade ago. It had been a quick and unkind goodbye. She'd said she wouldn't go to the launch party, refused his book, and she'd left.

"Paul, forget about what happened last night, okay? Pretend it was just some sort of screwed up alternate history."

"Alternate history? You think it's that easy to forget it?"

"It can be." She stepped closer to him. "Do you *really* want to die?"

He took a breath, looked Alice in the eyes and then shook his head. "No."

"Good. Then we've got to find a way to..."

The flash was blinding and the roar of thunder followed immediately after. Sparks raged across Alice's flesh and she felt herself convulsing as she fell to the ground.

Auto-rewind.

Alice followed the same conversation she'd had before, but she started moving him immediately, asking him to walk with her the moment she saw him.

"Do you *really* want to die?" she asked.

He thought about it several seconds then said, "No. Not really. But to tell you the truth, Alice, the only reason I don't want to right now is because you're with me."

Something stirred in her gut. She didn't say anything.

"I can't stop thinking about you. I've tried, but it's like..."

A flash of lighting reflected off the glassy buildings and Alice knew it was the one that had killed him last time. She winced, thinking of the pain it had caused when it hit them. The thunder roared so loudly that neither one could speak for a few seconds.

"Paul," Alice interrupted. "Your life is in danger."

"It's just a storm," Paul said.

"No. It's not." She wanted to tell him everything, tell him he'd been poisoned so many times she didn't want to count, tell him that he would have been struck by lightning a moment ago if she hadn't made him move.

She thought about actually saying it all when the lightning struck a second time.

Auto-rewind.

14. THE

"It's just a storm."

Alice turned down the best block she had found so far. She'd been working this problem for a week's worth of time now and she still hadn't succeeded in getting him more than a quarter mile from the center of town before the disaster hit. The wind started to pick up, and her gut twisted up in knots.

"No. It's not just a storm." She knew she couldn't tell him the truth. Every time she had tried, she'd realized how crazy it sounded; that she could control time with her mind, that them falling in love had made her boss go nuts and start murdering him at every turn he took. She had never let the words come out, and she never would, but she might be able to lie.

"This storm isn't an accident. Someone wants to kill you."

"Kill me?" He laughed. "With a storm? Seems a bit melodramatic, doesn't it? Come on, Alice. *I'm* the writer."

"Yeah. And I'm the editor... for a *human* produced novel." She paused. Some part of her brain knew something about this timeline that didn't exist in the line she had originally come from. She said, "Humanity makes mistakes. Humanity lets the weather system fail. Humanity is weak and worthless."

Paul's face turned to worry. Everyone in this timeline had heard of Terror of Human Error, or THE as they were called. It was a terrorist group, dedicated to relieving all human beings of any work that a machine could do instead.

"You think THE caused this storm?" Paul asked.

Alice nodded. If he thought someone was actually trying to kill him, he might listen to what she had to say.

"That's crazy. No one is trying to kill me."

Perfect timing. Alice glanced around once to make sure they were in the right position then she said, "Oh no?"

Paul glared at her. "No."

She calmly reached out and pulled him back, just as a metal park bench crashed to the ground where he'd been a moment earlier.

Paul screamed and jumped further from the near accident. He looked up, as did Alice, to see the floating park was tipped sideways in the wind.

A tree finally tore free from the soil and started falling.

"Move," Alice stated, and Paul started running.

"No. Stop, Paul!"

He didn't stop soon enough. A RAT barreled by just as he stepped out into the street.

15. Final

"Let's move," Alice said, "Cautiously, please."

She kept her eyes open. Most things were the same between timelines, but stuff could change all the time. They got to the street and hailed a RAT.

It was dangerous getting into a transport, Alice realized that, but she had to get him out of the city before the space elevator came down. Some part of her wanted to run out of timelines in this awful storm series, but another part of her didn't. She had a feeling this series was the only set of lines Paul had left. If she couldn't get him to safety soon, he'd be dead. Completely dead.

They crossed Liberty street. Alice had survived after the elevator fall enough times to learn that it didn't damage anything East of Liberty street. She needed to get Paul home, and they were still several blocks from there. She debated a moment whether she should stop the RAV and get out, or just keep going. Get them a little closer.

She didn't say anything, and she put her hands on her knees, squeezing until her knuckles went white.

"Hey." He put a hand on hers, "What are you so worried about?"

She looked at him, took a breath...

And then the other car ran a red light and slammed into her RAT.

Alice had set several auto-rewind places so she wouldn't have to keep getting through the same dangers twice. She didn't have long to get back in the RAT, and as soon as it crossed Liberty street, she commanded the transport to stop. She tapped her ring and sent payment to the driver as they got out. They only took a few steps before several shots rang out.

Alice dropped to that familiar pain of a gunshot wound.

A small mob of people came out of hiding, stripping Alice and Paul of anything they had that could be of some value.

She looked at Paul. The shot that had taken him was more deadly than the one that hit Alice. The blood had drained from his face and he stared blankly up at the dark sky as rain fell all around him.

He gasped his last two breaths and then lay still.

Alice recognized this death. She had seen this death before. Josiah had showed it to her what felt like a thousand lifetimes ago.

It was one of his last.

She *had* to get him home. She *had* to keep him safe.

Rewind.

They went further than Liberty street, but stopped before the car accident could happen.

Alice got out of the RAT and Paul followed. "Where are we going?" he asked.

Alice knew what the final line held for her. They were getting close to it, but she knew what she had to do. "To your place."

He looked confused. "Then why don't we just stay on the RAT?"

Alice didn't want to get crushed in another accident. She shook her head. "It's safer to walk."

"Safer? On a day like this? You're the one who keeps telling me I shouldn't have come out here."

"You shouldn't have. But now I've got to get you back, so just ease up on me will you? I'm trying to save your life here. At least one of them."

He chuckled. "What?"

Alice realized her mistake and started walking. "Nothing."

By the time he caught up to her his face was serious. "No. What did you just say?"

Alice glanced at her watch. "We need to hurry."

"Alice." He stopped. She instinctively searched the surrounding area for any threats, but threats weren't necessarily something she could see before they happened. Lightning for instance. She didn't want to get struck by lightning again.

"Tell me the truth."

She couldn't rewind. If she did, she would leave this version of Paul, and he would probably end up dying. What if this was the last one? There was no way to tell, and his life was too precious to give it up just to avoid one stupid mistake she'd made.

She tried once more to change the subject. "Just come with me, Paul. Please."

"I'm not moving until you tell me the truth."

Paul was telling the truth. Alice knew he would recognize the truth from a lie. She had no choice left.

"I have the power to... reverse time."

"Reverse it?"

Alice nodded, even though she knew it wasn't as simple as a reversal. "Change it.

Try to make things better."

"Really?" Paul asked.

"Yes. Really."

Paul looked disgusted. "You try to make things better? I don't think screwing with time in order to make something better is a great idea."

Alice's heart stuttered. "What do you mean?"

"You take one individual action that you think will make things better, and maybe that action sets off a chain of events that makes everything else awful."

The Darkers had been making the universe better for a long time now. Alice shook her head. "They know how to isolate things."

"Isolate things?" he shivered visibly. "Are they going to isolate me?"

She thought of what Robertson was doing, killing every version of him except the one that didn't get to stay with Alice. She bit her lower lip. "They're going to try." She took a deep breath then said, "But your situation is a lot different than most people's involved in this."

"It's different? Why is that?"

Alice almost blurted out, *Because I love you*. Instead she said, "Because you're in an ever-fail."

Paul seemed to feel the weight of that word. He almost sounded reverent as he asked, "What's an ever-fail?"

"It's a phenomenon, where every single choice you make leads to your death."

"You mean I'm going to die?" he asked, innocently afraid.

Alice almost cried. "You already have, Paul! A hundred times. A thousand times. I can't even count it anymore!"

He took a step toward her. "What about you? Are you going to die?" His voice was low with concern.

The breath locked up in her lungs a moment before she lied. "No. Not if I can get you to safety."

A deafening noise filled the air. It was more like a thousand noises; the screeching of metal, shattering glass, mortar snapping away from the bricks it used to hold in place. The screams of anyone nearby.

"Crap!" Alice exclaimed. "Run. Go!"

They raced away from the falling space elevator. Alice refused to look back. So many times she had been caught in that disaster, yet she'd been dumb enough to let Paul stand there, just outside the danger zone while they chatted about time.

Part of the elevator shattered behind them with a force so hard it blew Alice's hair forward despite the fact that it was soaking wet. She didn't stop. She kept running.

Until she heard Paul's voice behind her. "Alice!"

She spun around to see him on his hands and knees, struggling to keep himself upright, struggling to keep from falling.

A beam from the elevator had speared him straight through.

Alice ran back, reaching him just before he fell to his side.

"This just... another... one of my... deaths?" He forced a laugh through the pain.

Alice's TCC flashed a warning that they would be transferring to the final line at the termination of the choice.

A tear slipped from Alice's eye. "Yeah. Another one of your deaths," she said, then shook her head. "Your last one."

"You mean... not coming back?" His face read like a horror novel.

"No. No. You're coming back," she whispered. "You're coming back, and you're living."

He relaxed. The news she'd given him

seemed to ease some of his pain almost. He sighed and closed his eyes. "I want to live with you."

Alice couldn't hold it in any longer. She started sobbing.

Paul opened his eyes and looked at her. The question burning in his gaze.

Alice shook her head. "You won't live with me, Paul. I'm your Natalie. I'm your tragic heroine."

"No," he whispered.

"Yes. It's how it has to be. You live..." She licked her lips, tried to breathe through the series of sobs that followed. "And I die."

"How?"

She told him.

Tears poured from his eyes. He struggled to take a breath. "*No,*" the word was so quiet she could barely hear it above the sound of rain pounding the ground. "*Alice. Don't you let... don't...*"

He closed his eyes and there were no more forced breaths. He was silent and still. He was dead.

For the very last time.

Alice curled into a fetal ball and sobbed into her hands. There was a choice for her to make. If she didn't rewind, she could live. But if she took this line, she would have to live without Paul.

If she went back, took that final line then she would die. But Paul would live.

She lifted her head, looked at his body, pushed the tears from her eyes.

"Rewind."

The word tasted bitter as she said it.

16. Natalie

They got out of the RAT, far enough past Liberty street that they wouldn't get killed by the muggers, and before they went through the intersection and got smashed by an idiot driver.

"Where are we going?" Paul asked.

"To your place.

Confusion read across his face. "Then why don't we just stay on the RAT?"

"Because if we did, we'd get killed."

Paul chuckled, then his face turned serious. "What?"

She knew if she told it to him straight that he wouldn't believe her, but if he asked her to tell him, then he would. "Nothing." She kept walking.

Paul caught up to her, his face serious. "No. What did you just say?"

Alice glanced at her watch. She looked up to the distant space elevator that would be falling soon. "We need to hurry."

"Alice." He stopped. "Tell me the truth."

Perfect. What she needed. "All right, I will," she said, then she put a hand on his back and urged him forward. "Just, while we're walking, please."

They had the same conversation. She could reverse time, make things better. Paul didn't think you *could* make things better by screwing with time.

Alice avoided the word isolation. "Maybe you're right," she said. "Maybe everything they're doing won't make anything better. But I've got no choice but to keep you safe now, Paul."

"Keep me safe?" he slowed his walk, but Alice urged him on. He picked up the pace again and looked at her. She could read something in his face. Recognition perhaps. Maybe he was experiencing deja vu. "Am I going to die?"

Alice shook her head with determination. "No," she said. "No. You're not."

The cacophony of the elevator falling sounded behind them, and Paul spun around in terror. Alice paid it little attention. She had been much closer to that noise many times before. The distance they were at made it sound like it was nothing at all. There would be no spears of metal to impale Paul, no falling debris to crush him, no maniacs waiting in the alley to kill him. He would make it. This time, he would actually make it.

And then it was Alice's turn.

They reached Paul's home and Alice checked the street to make sure there were no cars coming. "Let's go," she said, pulling him after her as they jogged up the stairs.

Paul unlocked the door and they went inside. Alice shut and locked the door behind her. Not that it would do her any good. The final threat wasn't coming from outside the physical world. Her final threat was coming from outside time, and there were no door locks for that.

They went into Paul's living room and Alice dropped down on the couch, completely exhausted; mentally, physically, emotionally. She was drained. She had given absolutely everything.

Almost.

She hadn't given her last life. Not yet.

"So that's it?" Paul asked as he dropped down beside her. He'd grabbed a towel from the kitchen and he shuffled it through his hair. "All we had to do was get me home? Seems pretty simple."

"Simple." Alice let out a long, loud, "Ha!" then looked away from him.

"I'm sorry," Paul said, putting a finger under her chin and turning her face toward him. He wiped away some of the water on her face that was dripping from her hair. "I'm sure you've been through hell."

She looked into that face. She could read concern, deep care. She could read a touch of passion, and a lot of love. It made her want to cry, but she wasn't going to spend the last moments of her life sobbing like an idiot.

Pretend it will never end, she told herself. She leaned in and kissed him.

Paul slid his hands around her back, pulling her onto his lap. He held her close, breathing in deeply.

Alice closed her eyes, lost herself in the moment.

"Alice," Paul said in between kisses.

"Hmm?"

"I love you," he whispered.

Heat rushed through her body and she smiled. She loved hearing that from him. And now there was nothing to fear, no reason to hold back. "I love you, too, Paul."

"I'm sorry."

She sat up so she could see his face, but she couldn't read it. "Sorry? What do you..."

He shook his head. "You're not Natalie."

Paul shoved Alice to the side a mere instant before Robertson slipped out of time. Robertson was already swinging his knife, but instead of going into Alice's back like it should have, it went into Paul's chest.

"No! Paul!" Alice screamed. She rammed her shoulders into Robertson's legs, knocking him to the ground. She wanted to scream at him, but he looked to be in shock. He wasn't getting up, wasn't attacking her again so she turned back to Paul, twisting her ring to signal an emergency.

The blood was oozing around the blade of the knife. "No. What... what are you doing?" she cried. "How did this happen?"

"You told me you were going to die," he said. "You said you were my tragic heroine. Told me exactly how it would happen."

"How can you remember?" she asked, stunned. She thought of what Robertson had said, that things in one timeline often affect things in another.

Paul shook his head, pain screaming from the expression on his face. "I have enough tragic heroines with Natalie. Maybe if Raynes had made a few more of his own sacrifices... he wouldn't have wound up so alone."

"No, Paul. This isn't fiction. This is..." she shook her head. Tears fell from her cheeks. "This was my last chance to save you."

He smiled. "And my *only* chance to save you."

"You idiot," Robertson's deep voice rumbled. He got to his feet and looked between Alice and Paul. "If he dies, the future will..."

"If you were so worried about the future you shouldn't have started this ever-fail in the first place."

"Alice," Paul said. She looked at him. "If *you* were Raynes..."

Alice's heart crashed against her chest. Robertson told her he had never read *A Failure of Futures*. He knew how Natalie died—stabbed in the back—but he didn't know what Raynes did right afterward.

She shook her head. "No. It will kill you."

"Kill me faster, you mean. No one's coming to help. Not with this storm."

Alice looked over her shoulder to see Robertson still standing there, still moving through time like the rest of them. If she was going to kill him, this would be her only chance. Josiah had already told her she couldn't kill someone when they were outside of time, and Robertson only went into the flow of time on rare occasions. This was one of them.

Alice looked at him. He had backed several feet away from her. He was smart.

But not smart enough.

Stop.

Time froze. Alice jerked the knife from Paul's chest, put the towel over the wound and moved his hands into position so he could keep pressure on it.

She covered the distance in three steps, and then unpaused time.

"Wait, Aliss—"

She drove the knife through his heart and turned away as he fell.

"Paul!" she cried, dropping beside him on the couch. He was pressing down on the towel, but it was already soaked through with blood.

He had gasped at the pain of having the knife torn from his chest. Alice had seen him die thousands of times. She had gotten herself through it by always saying there was another Paul still alive somewhere.

This time was the last one. Paul was bleeding to death on his couch.

She couldn't watch it happen again. She wouldn't!

Stop.

She looked around the quiet,

motionless room, but there was nothing there for her. Robertson was dead, and Paul would be soon.

"Take me to Darkness." She hesitated, "To Josiah. If he still exists."

For some reason Alice expected chaos. Everyone would be scrambling to find some way to save Paul. No one was there. The halls were empty. Perhaps the TCC had just taken her anywhere in Darkness because Josiah didn't exist anymore. He didn't remember his grandmother, and now his grandfather was on a couch with a knife wound in his chest.

A door opened down the hall and a man stepped out, heading away from her. She recognized the familiar dark hair, the tall, almost lanky build. Josiah.

Alice jogged after him and called his name.

The man stopped and looked over his shoulder and Alice slowed. She'd thought it was him but she wasn't so sure now.

His whole face was covered in black bruises. His eyes were bloodshot, and his bright blue eyes were the same color gray as the walls. The shape of his jaw, his nose, his cheekbones were different too.

"Josiah?" she asked, shaking her head

as if she didn't believe she was speaking to the same man.

"Uh. Yeah..." he sounded exhausted.

"What happened to you?"

He scoffed. "Genetic shift. It kind of..." he winced, "No, it *really* hurts."

Alice shook her head. "It's all because of me."

"Could be." He squinted at her. "Who are you?"

Alice swallowed a lump in her throat. "Alice," she said. "Alissandra Goetz."

Josiah frowned. "Sorry. This shift is really screwing with me."

"You don't remember me?"

"I don't remember much. They say it will get better when the change is complete." He looked at Alice a moment. She could still almost read his face and she was pretty sure he was feeling a tiny bit of recognition. "How can I help you?" he asked.

"We spoke before," Alice said. "Your..." she almost said grandfather, but stopped herself. "My subject was in an ever-fail. He should have lived, and I should have died in the final line, but..." it was hard to breathe for a few seconds, so she quit trying. "That didn't happen. Now he's bleeding out and there's nothing I can do for him."

Josiah stared at her. "You seem so familiar."

"It doesn't matter now. I just need your help again. I didn't know where else to go." Something tickled her cheek and she brushed away a tear. "The paramedics won't get there in time. I don't know what to do. I *can't* let him die."

"Well..." he trailed off. "When are you from?"

She bit her lip. "Publication of *A Failure of Futures*. Do you remember that book?"

He blinked several times. "Yeah. I read that thing since I was a kid... I think?"

"You have to help me," she begged.

He put a hand to his forehead and sighed with exhaustion. "He's bleeding?"

Alice nodded.

"Can you put a bandage on it?"

Maybe he wouldn't be as much help as she had thought. "No. I don't think a bandage would do it."

Josiah frowned and shook his head. "This wouldn't even be a concern if he was alive in another couple hundred years from your time, but... I'm sorry. I'm not a doctor. I can't think of what you—"

"What do you mean it wouldn't be a concern?"

He shrugged. "You'd just fill it up with MediPlast. Maybe give him a blood transfusion if he need—"

"Get me some."

Josiah's eyebrows folded together. "It's from your future. Giving it to you in the past would be illegal."

"What Robertson did was probably illegal, too. If you knew all the illegal things I've done in the last few hours..." she reached out and took one of his hands in hers. "Please, Josiah. He's your..." she debated if she wanted to say this. "He should be your grandfather."

Josiah looked down at the ground. He chewed his lower lip a few times then nodded. "Just wait a thought," he said, and disappeared.

A moment later he showed up again with a small gray tube in his hand. "The MediPlast will stop the bleeding and sanitize the wound, but you're going to need to get him a blood transfusion as soon as you can."

Alice reached for the MediPlast but he pulled it back and looked down at it. He frowned.

"Find a doctor that won't ask questions." He shook his head. "Don't let anyone even see the wound, you understand?"

Alice nodded. "I understand."

Josiah finally relented and handed the tube over. Alice took the MediPlast from him like it was priceless. "Thank you," she whispered.

She started to leave and he said, "Alice. Why do I know you?"

She smiled. "I might be your grandmother."

She didn't wait for his reaction. Even though time wasn't moving for Paul, all she wanted was to get back to him. When she reached Paul and slipped into time, he was drawing rasping breaths. His hands still clutched the towel to his chest, but he was losing strength.

"Let me see." Alice demanded.

His hand fell to the couch and his eyes drifted closed. Alice ripped the shirt open and squeezed the MediPlast into the wound.

Some part of her wanted Paul to be just fine, right then. Wanted him to jump up and say that he felt better. As she looked into his pale face she could see that he had lost consciousness. She needed to get him a transfusion, but she didn't know how she would ever find a doctor who would agree to not look at the wound. Her TCC was telling her Paul was still alive, along with it griping about all the rules she was currently breaking. Whatever. Robertson had probably broken his own score of rules, and he'd pay for it when the Darkers resurrected him from some other line.

There was a knock at the edge of the room, but it wasn't coming from the front door. Alice snapped to attention, looking up to see Josiah standing just inside the room, carrying a case. "Can I come in?" he asked.

The bruises were gone. His face had returned to something similar to what it had been when they first met, but it was subtly different. She couldn't tell how.

"Yes," she said. She looked down at the mess she was, covered in blood, probably pale from the shock. "You're looking better," she said.

Josiah nodded. "It's been almost a year for me. I had to get special permission to come back here."

That was so strange to Alice. She had seen him just seconds ago, but he was from a different time. He could go whenever he wanted to. If it had been a year, he knew things. "Do I get in big trouble?"

"You get in a little trouble," he took a few steps forward and glanced at Robertson's body. "But the Darkers felt that you had little choice but to do what you did. And while the future wasn't exactly what they expected it to be, it did turn out acceptable."

He walked over and sat down next to Paul, opening the case and bringing out a bag of blood. He started a transfusion. Alice relaxed for a moment and then tensed up again when she thought of what had happened.

"I'm sure Robertson's going to be unhappy with me when they bring him back from another universe."

"Robertson is dead."

Those words hit Alice like a punch in the gut. She hated the fact that she'd had to kill him, but it was just like all the other times Paul had died. She knew there were more of him. "There's other versions of him elsewhere," Alice said. "Just like everyone, other timelines he's alive on."

Josiah made a look of pity then said, "Not Robertson. He took his last mission too far, lost too many lines. He was a lot like you, Alice. Only one version of him left.

Didn't you ever wonder why he never went into time?"

"Oh." Alice couldn't say she was sorry to hear that. She wasn't really.

"The Darkers were able to isolate Paul in his final line as well. They removed him from the space elevator catastrophe. If he even remembers it at all, it will only be a vague dream or some wild imagination."

"And me?" Alice asked. "Did they isolate him from me as well? Turn me into a dream?"

Josiah didn't say anything. He checked a monitor he had set on Paul's chest. Alice was still kneeling in front of Paul, but she moved to sit on the corner of the coffee table across from Josiah instead.

"It's easier to show you than to tell you," he said, and transferred the memories to her TCC.

Alice watched it with that haze that always came when seeing the future. She saw Paul on the stands, giving motivational speeches. Paul at his Lillypad, writing a new novel. Paul with the editor...

An editor who *wasn't* Alice.

She nodded. "I suppose the future would have been fine without me. Robertson could have killed me instead of

Paul."

Josiah smiled at her. "That's the future everyone else sees. They see Paul alone his entire life, strong, intelligent... single. It's what the Darkers wanted. It's what's acceptable."

"Good. Fine," Alice said, feeling passive-aggressive. "As long as the Darkers get what they want."

Josiah was grinning at her.

"What?"

"As long as the Darkers get what they want, they don't care what happens behind the scenes, in the quiet moments where no one else can see. I suppose in other words, they don't care what happens in the darkness." He paused a full two breaths then said, "Watch."

She did. She watched Paul on the stands, giving a motivational speech. If Alice looked over his left shoulder she could see her face in the crowd. She watched Paul at his Lillypad, struggling to find the right words, and Alice coming up behind him, rubbing his shoulders, offering suggestions. She watched Paul work with the editor who wasn't Alice, then come home and go over the book again with her.

She watched Paul telling Alice her

metaphor is beautiful, Paul kissing Alice with the passion they had shared in only Alice's memory, Alice touching the scar on Paul's chest where a knife had tried to take him away from her.

She saw the marriage ceremony, performed in a small church on another timeline so there would be no record of it in the Universal Consciousness. She saw the stupid fights over stupid things, the apologies and the forgiveness.

She saw the children. The grandchildren; Josiah reading *A Failure of Futures*.

She saw Paul and herself growing old together, dying less than a week apart from each other.

"Last time I saw you," Josiah said as the images came to an end, "I said you were so familiar to me. Now that my memories have reformed, I finally know why."

Alice looked into his eyes. They were no longer that beautiful blue just like Paul had. They were light brown. So light they almost looked orange. Just like her own eyes.

Alice looked at Josiah again and nodded her head. "Thank you."

"No. Thank you, Alice. You had no idea this would turn out all right when you decided to die for him."

Josiah looked at the empty blood bag and pulled the needle out of Paul's arm. He cared for the small wound then glanced down at Paul. "He'll wake up soon. The Darkers couldn't remove his memories of what you told him like they did with the elevator. He knows about Darkness, and he always will. The both of you will always keep it secret."

"Oh great." Alice knew she was going to have quite a few discussions with Paul about the morality of what the Darkers were doing. The problem was, she would probably agree with Paul's opinion for the most part.

"I need that MediPlast back."

Alice handed him the tube and when he took it he held her hand in his for a few seconds.

"What?"

"You were my favorite grandma. It's funny, seeing you so young, me being so tall. I always had to look up to you."

Alice smiled at him. "The truth is, Josiah, I was probably looking up to you."

He took a deep breath and hugged her. "Bye, Grandma."

Alice didn't know if it was weird or

sweet that he was calling her grandma, but she knew even though grandparents weren't supposed to have favorites, she was already destined to have one.

She watched Josiah walk out and then she looked down at Paul. He was awake and staring up at her.

"Hey," she said quietly, sliding down to sit beside him.

"You look happy," he told her.

Alice nodded. "I am."

He tilted his head with genuine curiosity. "Why?"

"I saw something."

"And what did you see?"

Alice cuddled into Paul and kissed him on the cheek, daydreaming about everything they were going to share together.

"I saw an acceptable future."

The End

Note From the Author

Thank you for reading An Acceptable Future. Reviews mean the world to authors. If you enjoyed this book, please consider rating it and leaving a review with the review site of your choice. Visit my Amazon page at

www.amazon.com/stores/L.-P.-Masters/author/B01N51SSFD

About the Author

Born and raised in the rainy streets of the Seattle area, L.P. Masters spent her fair share of time staring out rain-streaked windows and writing books. Masters has always had extremely vivid dreams, which often spark inspiration for her novels.

In 1999, after one such dream, Masters began writing her first novel. She has participated in National Novel Writer's Month every November since 2010. Writing isn't the only thing she can do with a pen in her hand, she also enjoys sketching and drawing—with varying degrees of success.

Masters now lives in the slightly-less-dreary city of Spokane Washington with her husband, her three wonderful children, and a slightly neurotic poodle.

Acknowledgments

The first person I have to thank is my husband. I am continually amazed at the amount of time he spends listening to my ideas and giving me feedback. His help has been invaluable, especially in terms of this sci-fi universe that I have created. I'm sure that probably half of of this universe is thanks to him.

Also, my sister Kaylene, who got me thinking about writing choose your own adventure stories back in 2010. Although this novel is not choose your own adventure, thanks to Alice's TCC, which makes all the choices for her, future Dark Tale stories will be.

Thanks to Richard Baldwin who set the seeds for the myriad theories I needed to come up with in order to create Darkness and the multiple universes. Keep your eye out in future books for mention of the Baldwin Theory. It's the basis for everything that happens in the multiple universes.

And always I would like to thank my parents for their continued support and appreciation of my work. They have helped me in so many ways, and I don't think I will ever be able to say thank you enough.